The Stone Soup Book
of Fantasy Stories

The Stone Soup Book of

FANTASY

Stories

By the Young Writers
of Stone Soup Magazine

Edited by
GERRY MANDEL, WILLIAM RUBEL,
and MICHAEL KING

•

Children's Art Foundation
Santa Cruz, California

The Stone Soup Book of Fantasy Stories
Gerry Mandel, William Rubel, and Michael King, editors

Copyright © 2013 by the Children's Art Foundation

·

Stone Soup Magazine
Children's Art Foundation
P.O. Box 83
Santa Cruz, CA 95063

www.stonesoup.com

·

ISBN: 978-0-89409-027-1

Book design by Jim MacKenzie
Printed in the U.S.A.

Cover illustration by Anton Dymtchenko, age 13,
for "To Kill a Unicorn," page 11

About Stone Soup

Stone Soup, the international magazine of stories, poems, and art by children, is published six times a year out of Santa Cruz, California. Founded in 1973, *Stone Soup* is known for its high editorial and design standards. The editors receive more than 10,000 submissions a year by children ages 8 to 13. Less than one percent of the work received is published. Every story and poem that appears in *Stone Soup* is remarkable, providing a window into the lives, thoughts, and creativity of children.

Stone Soup has published more writing and art by children than any other publisher. With our anthologies, we present some of the magazine's best stories in a new format, one designed to be enjoyed for a long time. Choose your favorite genre, or collect the whole set.

Contents

The Faerie Circle

by Alana Yang, age 12

ARIEL WOKE UP at 11:55 p.m. She tossed off her blanket, stood up, and tied her favorite silver sweater around her waist. Silently, like a ghost, she slipped out the door and walked down the hallway. She could hear her sister Sophie breathing as she walked past her room. Down the stairs, skip the creaky third step, past the dining table, jump over Fluffy the greyhound (Sophie picked the name when she was six), and out the den door. Ariel didn't know where she was going, or why she was going there, but it felt... right. It felt like there was something she needed to do.

Moonlight poured down on the figure moving silently across the dew-covered lawn. Ariel knew this path by heart. She and Sophie went there years ago to play faeries, but they stopped when Ariel entered middle school. Now, as a seventh grader, she didn't feel the least bit embarrassed to be visiting one of her childhood haunts.

As Ariel's bare foot stepped into the moonlit clearing, she felt a thrum of... joy? Power? Memories? It felt like someone

Alana was living in Santa Rosa, California, when her story appeared in the March/April 2007 issue of Stone Soup.

THE STONE SOUP BOOK

was watching her. She glanced up at the moon and, as she always felt when she looked up at the sky, was awed by the great white disk sending down rays of milk-white light like so many chords of music.

Ariel slowly sat down across the clearing from the Faerie Circle that she and Sophie had played in. The ring of daisies never grew over, and the delicate white blooms always grew back whenever Sophie and Ariel had picked the flowers. Now the daisies were splashed lilac with moonbeams. Ariel sat and waited for Them. She had never seen Them before, but she knew that tonight was the night. They didn't let just anyone see Them.

Ariel glanced at her watch, pushing long black hair from her eyes. 11:58. Ariel shifted and promptly sat in a small puddle of water. It had rained during the day and the ground had little wet patches all over. Ariel peered into the shining liquid and saw her reflection—a thin pale girl with large violet eyes staring back at her. Ariel sat back and sighed. She wished her dark hair, now tipped with water, was capable of doing something other than just hanging straight around her face. And then she heard it. Or, rather, she didn't hear it. Everything went silent. Ariel looked at her wrist again. *Beep.* Twelve o'clock. Midnight.

Sparkling points of light poured by the dozens from the grand old oak tree at the edge of the clearing. Slowly, the Faeries appeared and sat on the daisies in the circle like chairs. Ariel could hardly breathe. The Faeries either didn't notice her or ignored her. They were indescribable in human words.

Each three-inch-tall Faerie had a shimmering dress in a color we do not have a name for. As the Queen sat down, her sheet of red corkscrew curls fanned out in an invisible breeze.

Then the Faeries slowly unfolded their wings, leapt into the air, and started to dance. Suddenly, they started to sing. The mixture of the Faeries' dance and their singing, so like angels' voices, was... incredible. It was moonbeams, light, the sun, stars, the four elements—water, fire, wind, and earth. It was rainbows and poetry. It was more than all of that. It was Magic. Pure and indescribable Magic.

It felt like they danced for years, but finally, they drifted back down to the Faerie Circle. Ariel was shaken out of her trance as each Faerie picked her daisy, and they arranged them in a pattern on the dirt. The Queen took her own beautiful daisy and placed it in the pattern, then made a call, like a bird, to the other Faeries. Ariel held her breath. It was over.

The shimmering Faeries flew back as softly as they had come— little orbs of shining light—and that is when Ariel dared to move. She looked at her watch. *Beep.* One o'clock.

Suddenly curious, she moved to a standing position to look at the pattern the Faeries had created.

Her eyes widened when she saw her name, Ariel, spelled out in daisies, with the Queen's own pulsing daisy for the dot on the *i*. A breeze swept over Ariel's arms as she bent to pick up the Queen's daisy. As she watched, the daisy disappeared, and in its place lay a gold chain with a pulsing, glowing, shimmering, iridescent pendant. The pendant was a capital *F* with Faerie wings.

Ariel sighed with joy.

She had watched the Faeries dance at midnight on the full moon.

She had been accepted.

She was one of Them now.

To Kill a Unicorn

by Abbie Brubaker, age 12

OUR SMALL HUNTING party trotted silently along the woodland path, searching for the white ghost of the forest. We knew the unicorn's weakness now. An old enchanter, passing by my father's castle, had said that a maiden fair of face could trap a unicorn with a golden bridle. We were taking along Jaif's younger sister, Francesca, for that job.

The party was speeding up, making its way quicker now, for we were few. Francesca and her father, who was the Earl of Keshry, Jonathan the dog-keeper and his three finest hounds, me, and my own father. Francesca rode behind the Earl on his gray charger, while I had my own horse: a rather slow brown mare. Jonathan walked, holding the dogs' taut leashes, and Father brought up the rear on a fine black stallion. I looked around, taking in the forest scenery, and knowing that a unicorn would have trouble hiding its snowy fur among the trees. Suddenly, the dogs stiffened and began to bay, nearly startling me off of my horse.

Abbie was living in Lancaster, Pennsylvania, when her story appeared in the May/June 2007 issue of Stone Soup.

"They've scented the creature," muttered Father to Jonathan. "Quiet them now. They'll frighten it deeper into the woods." He turned on his horse to face me. "Matthew, take Francesca into the meadow, then come back to us. We'll wait in the trees until the unicorn is trapped, then Jonathan will let loose the dogs to keep it in place until we get there. Understood?" I nodded. Father tossed me the heavy golden bridle. Then the Earl let Francesca down off his horse, and I helped her onto mine. She raised a hand in farewell to the remainder of our hunting party, then we disappeared into the trees. I knew the way to the meadow, so it was very easy to let my mind wander from guiding my horse. It had been about two minutes riding, before a voice broke the silence.

"Do you really think I should do it?" I was surprised to hear Francesca's question.

"Do what?" I asked, looking sideways at her serious face.

"You know, catch this unicorn. They've always sounded so noble to me, and I don't think I want to help kill one."

I started to reply, but the trees ended and we were in the meadow. I let Francesca down without answering, and began to turn my horse, but she hissed, "The golden bridle, Matthew!"

Uh-oh. I retrieved the bridle from my saddle and handed it down. Then I nudged my brown mare and backed into the forest again. Once hidden behind a sufficient number of trees, I turned to watch.

Time passed. I had long since picked out Father's hiding place, and also that of the Earl. The unicorn had not come yet. How long would we wait? My horse stomped her feet and whinnied softly, and I rubbed my hand along her velvety muzzle.

"Shhh, girl. Quiet now," I murmured. She didn't understand why we were to stand here for hours on end. Come to think of it, I didn't really get it either. All this fuss and bluster, for the sake of killing a rare and beautiful animal. Then suddenly—oh, my. I saw it.

The unicorn stepped from the forest, shedding bits of leaves and thorns. Its long horn glistened as though polished to a shine. I saw at once why many men chased after it—the creature was so wondrous. Francesca looked up sharply. I could see her hands trembling, clenched around the golden strands of the bridle. The unicorn warily turned its head in my direction, and I almost met its deep brown gaze. But, the thought of looking into the eyes of something you are about to help kill—I quickly glanced down at the ground. It can't see you, Matthew. Don't worry about it.

The white apparition trotted to stand in front of Francesca, and lowered its head. My heart was pounding, and I watched as the girl reached up and placed a hand on the unicorn's mane. Would Francesca be able to do it? Her other hand still held the bridle. The Earl, I saw, was waving impatiently at his daughter, sending a silent message. The bridle! Now!

My horse had stopped moving, and stared at the unicorn with simple wonder. I was staring just as wondrously, struck by the sudden thought that Father and the Earl were going to kill it.

Francesca grabbed the golden bridle in both hands. She began to bring it up towards the creature's head; I heard the Earl give a quiet chuckle of delight, but I couldn't bring myself to be triumphant. Had I really set out with a will to murder the rarest animal in the forest? I wanted to tell myself no, I hadn't, but I wasn't sure. At least now I was of a clear conscience. The unicorn wouldn't die by my hands, I swore silently. Father's face, half hidden in shadow where he was concealed, was smiling, the smile of the hunter who has his prey in an inescapable trap.

But no! The unicorn wheeled and ran suddenly, leaving Francesca to sink to the ground. She had whispered something in the creature's ear, I was sure of it, told it that it would die if it stayed. With a cry, the Earl signaled to Jonathan to release the dogs. My heart, which had risen so suddenly, plummeted again. The hounds would catch the unicorn, bring it down in a bloody scene of horror. The Earl signaled again, but Jonathan hadn't let go of the leashes. He held them in a white-knuckled grip, his face stony.

"Jonathan!" Father snapped. "We're losing time!" The dog-keeper shook his head, slowly walking back to stand beside me.

"M'lords, face it," he said softly, "none of us can kill a unicorn." He gestured at Francesca, on her knees in the meadow; to me, leaning against an elm tree for support; and to his own paled face. Father cursed, mounting his horse and gesturing to the Earl to do the same. I took the reins of my mare and led her into the meadow.

"Francesca?" I asked hesitantly, not sure what she would say. She stood up unsteadily, and gave me a sad smile.

"It's not dead. That's all I could do for it." Without another word, I helped her into the saddle. After I had mounted, we joined Father and the Earl on the edge of the clearing. Jonathan came up beside us, his three dogs sniffing and whimpering with confusion. Francesca shot her father a look that was steely edged, and my father did likewise to me. In frosty silence, our hunting party set off, heading towards home. Jonathan looked at me and smiled.

"I think we've all learned something," he said. "A life as rare as that one isn't easily taken."

I nodded, adding, "And any life is hard to take."

A Girl Called Helena

by Rachel Cohen, age 12

IT HAD TO BE the worst storm the town of Seaport, New Jersey, had ever experienced. The rain struck the earth like pins piercing a pincushion, so keen and strong that there was only a foggy sheet of gray encircling the ocean. Flashes of lightning brightened the sky, and thunder sounded all around. Wind swarmed, howling at the ocean and tumbling through the air, sending a chill through our house. Behind it, the mangled ocean tangled with the thunderstorm. Even the stars and moon were shielded by opaque, blackening clouds.

Meanwhile, I, Linda Fortinger, sat trembling by my bedroom window. I was wearing lavender fleece pajamas. Covering my quivering shoulders with the orange sheets on my bed, I peered out into the gloom from my bedroom window. I heard my younger sister, Kaitlyn, snoring from across the room, honey-blond waves scattered on her pillow, and my parents sleeping silently in the next room over. I was alone, too awed to sleep, to tear my eyes from this scene.

Rachel was living in Swarthmore, Pennsylvania, when her story appeared in the March/April 2006 issue of Stone Soup.

In my eleven years of life, I had never seen the ocean like this, a wave of fury fighting, an angry mob rampaging through the streets. The ocean was my only friend here on vacation in New Jersey. I swam by its shores, surfed along its waves, sailed its surface, but never saw it in a frenzy.

And then I saw it. My eye caught a blurry silhouette emerging from the ocean. As I squinted to get a better look, I saw the figure slowly bob to the surface and glide toward the sandy beach. I gasped in fright. No, it couldn't be... I rubbed my eyes, and the figure had disappeared.

I lay back on my bed, amazed. I assured myself it was only a wrecked sailboat, or perhaps an unlucky sea creature. Maybe my eyes were fooling me. I couldn't bring myself to believe it, but I was sure I saw, through the darkness, the profile of a girl, with a shadowy stream of black hair tossing in the wind behind it.

"LINDA! COME DOWN to breakfast, dear, it's nearly nine o'clock!" At the sound of my mother's voice, I rose hesitantly from bed, thrust on a lime-green T-shirt and denim shorts, brushed my hair and teeth, and went downstairs to the kitchen.

There, my mother was bustling over by the stove, her brown ponytail skipping along with her, adding brown sugar to my hot cereal. Kaitlyn sat at the table, stirring her own cereal with one hand, and holding her dainty head with the other. My father had apparently already left; an empty bowl lay on his placemat. He was probably down the street fixing the Fervents' old fence or down at the old boardwalk, nailing stray boards into place; he was an engineer and was always volunteering for something or other. I pulled out a stool and sat, glancing at the small television in the middle of the table.

"Here you go, sweetie," my mother smiled heartily, handing me a bowl of hot cereal. "Now girls, today I was planning that we could spend the morning at the beach, then try this new Asian restaurant at the end of town. After that, we're free to do anything, unless your cousins in Ocean City call us... Anyway, I was hoping that—oh no, not another one!" Her head was turned to the television, announcing that a certain Hurricane Helena was likely to travel northwest from its current perch in the Atlantic Ocean and hit New Jersey in about a week.

"These storms... just all popping out of nowhere, and on vacation, too! Now we might have to go grocery shopping this afternoon instead..." my mother grumbled, clearly annoyed. She began to slice a peach in silence. I simply gulped down my cereal.

"Well, it looks as though some new folks are moving into the Melbournes' old shack," Kaitlyn piped up. It was true; moving vans were parked along the road, and many people were unpacking sofas and mattresses and bureaus, heaving them through the open door. This was good news; the Melbournes were an old, quiet couple who lived across the street from our beach house in an unkempt two-story house that wasn't in very good condition for a house right next to the ocean. After Mrs. Melbourne died, her husband left the ocean, and for three years the building stood alone and untouched, until now.

"Let's go watch!" Kaitlyn suggested eagerly. The pair of us trotted across the street, where the family was just getting settled.

A surge of envy filled me as I caught a glimpse of their daughter. She was beauty beyond belief, with shiny black hair that fell to her hips, a long sheet of dark silk. She wore a velvet magenta skirt that dragged behind her and a ruffled, white shirt. Then I saw her eyes flash toward me, blue-gray, with a hint of green and silver, identical to the ocean on a sunny day. My curiosity drew me closer.

"Hi," I muttered shyly, "I'm Linda Fortinger, and this is my little sister, Kaitlyn. We're staying for the summer at our beach house across the street."

"I see," the girl replied, in a tone so soft I could almost feel it. "I am Helena."

"Helena...?"

"Helena Crest. This is my mother, Lela, and my father, James. Pleased to meet you. I'm sure we'll become good friends."

Helena held out a tanned hand, and I took it.

"It's our pleasure." I grinned, my hopes rising. I've never found a true friend in these parts. "Well, I'd better get back home now. I'll see you later!" I dashed off across the street, too excited about my new neighbor to think about anything else.

"THIS IS HELENA. How may I help you?" a soft voice spoke into the telephone.

"Hello, Helena, this is Linda."

"Ah."

"Anyway, my mom is taking Kaitlyn out to buy a new pair of sneakers, so I was wondering if you'd like to take a walk along the beach with me."

"Oh, I'd love that!" the voice filled with excitement. "When will we?"

"How about I meet you there in five minutes?"

"Fantastic! Well, I'll see you in five minutes."

"Sure. Bye!" I hung up the phone and slipped into some flip-flops. When I trotted outside onto the front porch, Helena already stood waiting for me at the corner. Today, a lavender skirt blew along with the ocean breeze, rippling playfully at her ankles, and perched lightly on her shoulders was a white tank top.

"Let's go!" we said simultaneously, giggling as we ran up the creaky, wooden steps, and then onto the damp sand.

Helena and I walked down the coast in the water's fringe, collecting seashells and laughing merrily at the seagulls skimming the water's edge, hoping to catch a good fish for dinner. We even spotted dolphins dancing gracefully on the water and then diving down again.

"Linda, don't you love the ocean?" Helena said suddenly.

"Well yeah, it's a pretty nice place to be."

"Oh, no." Helena's shiny eyes peered straight into mine, and I felt the meaningfulness in her graceful expression. "Do you consider the ocean as an equal, as a faithful companion in life? Don't you ever feel that you're somehow tied to it, like a bond of friendship that is forever indestructible? I love the ocean, I always have, and I can almost feel the waves. Don't you agree?"

"Well... no," I admitted. "I mean, I never thought about it the way you do. I've liked the ocean, for surfing and swimming, and I've been coming here every summer since I was born, but the ocean is just there to me. I guess I'm not really tied to it like you are."

"Strange." Helena slowly turned to face the horizon, eyes darting toward the endless blue. "I would think that someone this close to the ocean, seeing that you came here since you were born, in one of the closest houses to the water, would feel the same. You grew up with the ocean, and yet you don't understand it." She paused, heaving a sigh. She looked up at the floating clouds, smiling faintly as if in a trance. "I just love it here, more than anywhere in the world. I love the way the waves are always lapping playfully at your toes, the soaked sand sinks into your heels, the way the waves tumble out to shore and seem to hug you with a gentle splash... speaking of which..." Clutching her skirt in two fists, she aimed a kick at me, and water splashed my new Bermuda shorts. I stood shocked for a moment, and then splashed her right back. Helena may have been plenty attached to the ocean, but she certainly knew how to have fun with it. We leaped and splashed all down the beach until we were so soaked and exhausted that our only choice was to go home.

IT WAS OFFICIAL. Helena and I were now best friends. We did everything together; rollerblade to the park, eat ice cream, and take walks on the beach. Over the next week, I had so much fun with her I didn't even realize the time flying by, and eventually, it did.

At the end of our first week of friendship, we were rollerblading home from the Dairy Queen. Still licking the strawberry ice cream off the ice cream cone, I was about to open the front door to my house when a voice from behind stopped me. It was Helena, shouting from her porch next door.

"Linda, wait!" she cried.

"What?" I queried.

"Before you go inside, I want to tell you something. I won't be seeing you for a while, but I want to say you've been a very good friend to me. By the way, get ready for the hurricane tonight. I heard it will be a rough one!"

"Oh… all right then," I replied. At that, a white, toothy smile glinted at me from Helena's porch. Then, my friend strolled to her front door and drew it closed behind her.

I remembered the hurricane. What had it been called? Hurricane… Hurricane…

Hurricane Helena! I gasped. "Helena!" I cried. The peeling white door remained closed, and no answer came. I assured myself it was only a coincidence. Then, without giving it a second thought, I rushed inside to prepare.

THIS STORM WAS much worse than the last. The rain began to pour when the sun would have set, if not for the looming clouds growing fiercer as the night wore on. The wind was starting to rage even before midnight, when the hurricane was scheduled to hit us. I shivered at the thought.

Once again, I sat awake at the window. Something had kept me awake, urged me here. All I saw was a dreary scene, and a drab sheet of black approaching once again. But there was something different, something unusual about tonight.

I was growing drowsy when I spotted a figure beyond the translucent curtain of gray. I gasped in horror and surprise. It was Helena.

She stood at the corner, where we usually met for a walk on the beach. She was wearing a bright red raincoat and a matching umbrella hoisted on her shoulder. But she couldn't fool me with a clever disguise. How well did I recognize that calm face, with such soft features, or that graceful gesture? I grew suspicious. Then, she turned, and began to walk away toward the beach.

I didn't care about getting wet, or getting in trouble. I

checked the clock; it read eleven o'clock. I had an hour, and I would have to use it wisely. Still in my lavender pajamas, I pulled a blue sweater over my head and a yellow raincoat on my shoulders quickly and quietly. Checking that Kaitlyn and my parents were all still fast asleep, I crept downstairs, and grabbed an umbrella and a flashlight from the kitchen. I took a deep breath and bounded through the door.

It was miserable, yes, and for a minute, I was sure I had been driven into insanity. But my determination was greater and more powerful than my fear, and with that in mind, I set out to find Helena.

I approached the beach and held my flashlight up to the sand. Long ago, a tractor had spread the sand smooth, and there was only one pair of footprints. I took my wet boot and set it next to the imprint of a shoe. They were the same size. I followed the footprints, which led only in a straight line. I suddenly stood still and found I had walked right up to the ocean. I glanced left, then right. There was no sign of Helena anywhere. But then where did Helena go?

As if answering my question, a group of dolphins were swaying in the waves. How could they be enjoying themselves when a vicious storm was about to hit? They leaped into a dive and threw themselves back under. I rubbed my eyes in panic. I saw it again exactly as it happened before. I could have sworn I had just seen a streak of pale peach among the blue skin of the dolphins, and long locks of black hair billowing out behind it. Comprehension dawned on my face.

Suddenly, an abrupt blast of wind knocked me over, and I jumped back up in alarm. The hurricane would hit anytime now. I darted back home just before the hurricane swooped down upon us.

"LINDA, HURRY UP! We have to leave in ten minutes. Kaitlyn, dear, don't try and carry that suitcase, your father will... Jonathan! Please come down now and pick up this suitcase of yours!

I'll grab some crackers for the ride home, and Linda, can you pick that up for me? Thank you, dear, you're a doll..."

Today we were leaving Seaport, New Jersey, to return home. For once in a lifetime, I would miss it. Last night, the night of the hurricane, was still fresh in my memory, and so was Helena. Speaking of the Crests, no one had heard of them since before last night; Mom said they probably left to avoid the storm; I didn't believe it. I dragged my suitcase to the car and loaded it into the trunk. My mother was in a rush to go, because we had to drive home and then go to our cousin Debbie's wedding in Philadelphia. Pretty soon, the family packed themselves into the car and drove off.

"So kids," my father chuckled, grinning at us through the rearview mirror, "Did you enjoy yourselves this year?"

There was a murmur of "Yes, it was fine," from Kaitlyn in the back seat.

But I whispered, so that only I could hear, "Oh, yes, we had tons of fun this year, Helena and I. I can hardly wait until next summer..."

Moon Child

by Brian Hoover, age 12

THE NIGHT AIR was crisp and cool upon Jake's face. Millions of tiny lights filled the sky like a field of fireflies. Like most nights, Jake sat on the old oak stump in the center of the silent woods. But tonight was special; he could feel it, the tension in the air, the stillness of the seemingly nonexistent wildlife. Something was to happen.

A warm breeze stirred the trees, their great green leaves shimmering in the moonlight. Jake looked up at the moon, he broke out in a grin and rose to his feet, the air before him shimmered like waves lapping at his bare feet. His ragged jeans hung loosely about his slender frame, his rough crop of midnight-black hair dancing in the breeze, his leather jacket dully reflecting the light from the iridescent moon. It was happening.

In the distance a lone wolf released its mournful cry, the forest around seemed to answer. All at once a great clamor arose as out of the trees broke hundreds of birds. Below them on the ground, picturesque white-tail deer, along with bears and foxes,

Brian was living in Bend, Oregon, when his story appeared in the July/August 2006 issue of Stone Soup.

ran away from the clearing. As soon as it had begun, it ended, and everything was still once more. They knew it was to happen.

The aurora of shimmering air encircled Jake, glittering around him like morning dew in the new sun's light. Jake stood stock-still, the grin gone from his face to be replaced by a look of awe, nothing like this had happened before in his lifetime, he knew nothing about what was going on, except that it was part of him, and that it was meant to be.

A loud, ear-splitting crack broke the silence of the night. Out of nowhere a blue-green bolt of lightning flew towards the earth at an astounding speed. Jake's body began to change, the smile had returned as he crouched on the ground. The bolt of lightning struck the ground not an inch before Jake's face. Fiery multicolored sparks flew, striking Jake all over. It was happening.

The ragged jeans and leather jacket fell away, along with the other articles of clothing, no longer necessary on this body of dense black fur. Jake lifted his new canine head and loosed such a howl that the very air seemed to vibrate with its melodious notes.

Jake turned, the shimmering air was gone, his time had come, as it now would for the rest of his life. He was a lycan, a demon, a werewolf.

Another call answered his, and he trotted off towards the reply. Above him the clouds parted, revealing a full blue moon. The Jake-wolf sat on his haunches, and howled once more at this sign of power. It had happened.

Time

by Kaija Warner, age 13

Chapter One

THOMAS WAS TEN years old and on a plane, a plane going to his grandparents' house on the shore of Lake Michigan. He hadn't seen his grandparents since his father's funeral three years ago. All he could remember was his grandpa smelled like apples and his grandma made delicious chocolate-chip cookies.

Thomas got off his plane at the airport. He took a taxi to his grandparents' address and had the driver drop him off at the beginning of the long winding driveway. He slowly dragged his suitcase up the driveway and found... nothing. It was as if there had never been a house there. Thomas did recognize the old dead oak, but for some reason, it was alive. Strange, but he was sure he was in the right place. Grabbing his suitcase, he ran back down the driveway, which was now nothing but dirt, rocks, and dead leaves. Thomas tripped and skinned his knee but got up and kept on running until he reached the road. It was now dirt with wagon ruts on either side. He saw the beginning of another

Kaija was living in River Falls, Wisconsin, when her story appeared in the March/April 2010 issue of Stone Soup.

driveway a little ways down the road to his left.

It took Thomas a short time to reach it and he walked up the flower-bordered drive. A stately white Victorian house appeared, enclosed within a wrought-iron fence. It looked very out of place. Thomas stepped through the gate, walked onto the porch and knocked. The door was answered by a red-headed girl about six years old wearing a white dress and a sash that matched her sea-green eyes.

"Um, e-excuse me, but could you tell me the date?" Thomas asked, somewhat afraid of the answer and unnerved by the way the girl was staring at him.

"It is June 15, 1908, of course!" she laughed.

This is not happening, Thomas thought. This only happens in movies or comic books! I'm dreaming. Yes, that must be it. Wake up! He pinched himself. It hurt. But wait a minute... this doesn't seem to be a dream because I can feel and smell and hear everything. It isn't fuzzy like my other dreams... so maybe this isn't a dream? He pinched himself again just to make sure.

"You're from the future, aren't you, Thomas. Two thousand four, to be exact," the girl said quietly. "And all you want right now is to get back to your grandparents' house."

"Yeah, but I don't see how that's possible," Thomas said. "Unless you know some magical way to time travel," he added sarcastically.

"My name is Charlotte, and yes, I do know a 'magical way to time travel.'"

Charlotte shut the door and skipped around the back of the house to the lakeshore. Thomas stood there, stunned, not sure if she was joking or if she actually could time travel. He decided it was worth a shot because he somehow trusted her. Thomas dropped his suitcase on the porch and followed her.

Down by the lake, the midafternoon sun was glinting blindingly off the water. Charlotte handed Thomas three pebbles she had picked up from the shore. How were pebbles going to get him back to 2004?

"Skip them while wishing as hard as you can to get back," she said cheerfully.

"But what happens if they don't work?" Thomas asked.

"Oh, don't you worry, Thomas. My pebbles will work, I guarantee it, just as long as you believe," she said confidently.

Slightly unsettled by Charlotte's certainty, Thomas skipped the first pebble. Nothing happened. He glanced at Charlotte, who smiled innocently at him, then skipped the second one. Again, nothing. Thomas was starting to wonder if he was going to be stuck in 1908 forever.

Gloomily, he picked up the last pebble. He threw with all his might, but the third stone came skipping back. It was shining with all the colors of the rainbow, flying back towards him. There was a flash of bright blue-green light and Thomas found himself standing on his grandparents' front porch with his suitcase.

Chapter Two

THOMAS'S GRANDPARENTS WERE, of course, happy to see him. They fussed over how much he had grown and asked what had taken him so long. Thomas mumbled something about delayed flights. His grandma, sensing that something was wrong, immediately fed him a plateful of warm chocolate-chip cookies and a glass of milk. Soon feeling better, Thomas put a Band-Aid on his skinned knee and helped his grandma with the dishes.

In his bed that night Thomas replayed his conversations with Charlotte in his head and noticed something that he hadn't before. She had known his name, the year he came from, and exactly what he wanted. How? Who was Charlotte? I'll bike down the road tomorrow and see if I can find her house, he promised himself as he drifted off to sleep.

At seven o'clock the next morning, Thomas wrote a note for his grandparents and dug the old bike out from beneath all the other junk in the garage. Coasting down the driveway, he turned left and pedaled hard up the hill until he found the spot where Charlotte's driveway had been. Now, it could not even be called an animal trail. Hopping off the bike, he walked up the trail until he found the fence, and beyond it, the house, still standing, if a bit overgrown and falling apart.

Leaning the bike against the fence, Thomas walked cautiously onto the wobbly porch and knocked on the door, half expecting Charlotte to answer it.

"Hello? Is anybody here?" he called, slowly forcing open the rusted hinges of the door and peeking inside.

"Um... Charlotte?" he whispered.

"Hello, Thomas." Charlotte's voice sounded whispery and seemed to come from everywhere at once. "I told you my pebbles work."

Chapter Three

THOMAS'S MOUTH FELL open. He was stunned. What was happening?

"Follow my ribbon, Thomas," Charlotte said.

Thomas noticed her sea-green sash draped across a coat stand. Suddenly, the sash twitched and started floating.

OK, this is definitely not normal, Thomas thought, but I trust Charlotte. She must have a good reason for this... maybe...

The sash fluttered down the once-grand hallway and into the dining room; there were dusty place settings arranged on the table. The elegant French doors slowly opened and the sash darted out and soared into the woods. Thomas dashed after it, attempting to dodge branches and undergrowth. After a few wild minutes, the ribbon stopped by an old stone fence.

Thomas halted, panting, and wiped at the scratches on his face, then realized that the stone wall was the border to a private cemetery. The ribbon beckoned him over to a small granite gravestone. Thomas knelt and read:

Charlotte Catherine Adams
April 5, 1902–June 16, 1908

THOMAS STARED at the blurry words as tears filled his eyes. He hadn't known Charlotte at all, but he felt like she was a little sister.

"Charlotte... w-where are you?" Thomas called. "Charlotte?"

"Thomas," said Charlotte's voice by his ear.

Thomas wiped his eyes and glanced up, and she was standing beside him, looking exactly the same as she had almost a century before.

"Charlotte, it says that you died the day after I came to your house. Did I do something that made you die?" Thomas whispered, hoping with all his heart that the answer was no.

"No, Thomas. It was a decision I made. I have to go now, but I wanted to say thank you."

"Thank you? For what?" Thomas asked.

"For believing. You won't be alone, I promise," Charlotte said, handing him a pebble. "Goodbye, Thomas."

"What? Charlotte, don't go!" Thomas pleaded.

But she just smiled and faded into the early morning mist.

"Bye Charlotte..." Thomas whispered to the open air.

Chapter Four

THOMAS SAT, FROZEN, for some time until the harsh caw of a crow startled him out of his trance. Stiffly getting up, he picked up Charlotte's now lifeless ribbon and put it back in his pocket along with the pebble. Thoroughly depressed, he decided to head back to his grandparents' house. Climbing onto his bike, he bounced back down the trail and onto the road, where he almost crashed into a red-headed girl picking wild blackberries by the side of the road.

Hearing the brakes squeal, the girl whirled around and

Thomas almost fainted. She looked exactly like Charlotte, right down to the blue-green eyes. Noticing his astonished expression, she smiled a gap-toothed smile, stuck out her juice-stained hand, and said, "Hi! My name's Lottie. Want a blackberry?"

And Thomas knew what Charlotte meant.

A Light Shining Out of the Darkness

by Jonathan Morris, age 12

ORION PADDED ALONG through the dense undergrowth, his leather-coated feet silent as death's cruel hand as they compressed the damp soil. His mother, Selena's, words, clear and simple as a raindrop, echoed through his head, "I need you to fill this basket with ashberries." Orion nodded, forgetting that his mother's words were only a reverie.

His elf eyes scanned the bushes, searching for the berries with the gray pallor. These berries were essential if he was to hold up his mother's reputation as the best healer in the Dawn Woods. Ashberries, his mother had only used them once in his presence. It was also the only time she had ever failed.

His father had gone out to hunt, a simple hunt out in the fairly safe Dawn Woods. No one knew that a young male dragon had made a home in a nearby cave where the deer had often lodged for the night. For all that was known, as his father had gone alone, he had entered the cave hoping to find the deer, there was something quite different waiting for him. The dragon

Jonathan was living in Grantham, New Hampshire, when his story appeared in the March/April 2008 issue of Stone *Soup.*

had appeared in front of him out of nowhere like a specter and unleashed a ball of burning hatred of all creatures at him and his horse.

Hours later his horse limped up to the small cottage and began to neigh. This awoke Selena who came warily outside to a gruesome sight. The beautiful white horse was filthy with ash and soot, its right flank was a different sight. A curling pattern of blood arched down its right flank. Wasn't white the color of life, not death? Dragging behind it was Orion's father holding on only by his foot, caught in a stirrup. His body was completely disfigured by oozing burns.

Selena had heaved him inside and into the room where she treated her patients. Orion had been out behind the house at the well, getting a drink of water. He was pouring the water into a cup when he saw his mother dragging the body through the house. "Who's that, Mommy?" he had drowsily questioned, staring at the unrecognizable body.

He had just barely been able to make out his mother's words, her voice was choked with tears, "Your father." It took a moment for his child's mind to register Selena's words, but when it did the effect was devastating for him. He broke down in silent tears at first; giving way to sobbing on the floor and wishing his father had heeded his words, begging him to stay home.

Selena had made a mush out of ashberries, the only known cure to dragonfire burns, and she began pasting her husband's figure with the bland-colored paste. Her tears were flowing freely now and were dripping on the raw-skinned body. Orion's father had then regained consciousness and the pain had driven him back into dreamful infinity. After hours of grief, the sun had risen, birds were tweeting, bugs were buzzing, but in the little operating room there was no life. The man's family came in full of hope, only to be sent back to the abject misery that had lasted the nearly endless night. Orion's father was buried in the woods, as was custom, for elves' home is the forest and to be sent off in any other way or buried in any other location would be obscene.

THE STONE SOUP BOOK

There had been no one but his own family to mourn his horrible demise, and Orion's home became a place of silent suffering.

Since then Selena had striven harder than ever not to let death arrive at her doorstep again. That morning it seemed that the fateful night had occurred again. A lone stranger arrived at their door in the same bedraggled condition as Orion's father had. Orion was surprised that the man was even conscious after his exhausting ordeal. He had brought the man in and Selena set to work. Selena opened the drawer labeled *Ashberries*. It was empty. In her franticness to save her husband, Selena had ravenously used up her entire store of the rare berries. In her grief over her beloved husband's death, she had not wanted to even look at the berries again, never mind refill her stash. Anyway, what were the chances that she would have to treat someone with dragonfire burns again? Orion was sent to retrieve the final but most important ingredient to the poultice that would save the man's life.

Now he was searching as best he could to keep the stranger from having the same fate as his late father. Finally, after what seemed like years of searching compacted into about an hour, Orion found the ashberry bush. Letting out a sigh of relief, he began to fill his basket.

When the basket was overflowing with the gray spheres, he began his trek home with celerity. He scampered through the door to the house, slamming it hastily behind him, and bore his precious cargo to his waiting mother. She dismissed him to his room at once, and Selena began crushing the berries with a pestle and mortar. Orion thumped onto his bed, exhausted after his long journey, and instantly fell into a dreamless slumber.

When he awoke, he immediately remembered the stranger and hurried into the kitchen. There, sitting at the table and tightly wrapped in bandages, was the man, smiling and happily conversing with Selena who, for the first time in years, was truly happy. The happiness that had hidden from sight for years in the midst of her sadness was finally showing itself, a light shining out of the darkness.

Behind the Curtain

by Dylan J. Sauder, age 13

THE OLD, WORN curtain loomed over the stage. Chairs covered in faded, red velvet cushions were scattered throughout the theatre. A piano that had once been played in the most famous of performances now housed a family of mice. The theatre was falling apart, yet it still contained a certain beauty and elegance. If you listened closely, you could faintly hear the soft, sweet sound of a violin coming from behind the dark curtain. A single candle on the glamorous chandelier that hung from the ceiling of the concert hall flickered to life. The violin was joined by a flute, clarinet, cello, and then a viola. As the instruments grew louder, the chandelier became brighter. Soon, the music of an entire orchestra floated throughout the theatre, and the hall was filled with the soft glow of candles.

Famous pieces by Tchaikovsky, Bach, Vivaldi, Beethoven, and many others were performed, yet the curtain never rose to reveal the mysterious musicians who played for an invisible audience. Just as soon as the music began, the harmonic sounds began

Dylan was living in Franksville, Wisconsin, when his story appeared in the January/February 2010 issue of Stone Soup.

drifting into the darkness, until only the lone violin could be heard; that, too, soon grew quiet.

Who were the mysterious performers whose music was so captivating? Who were they that hid behind the curtain of the abandoned concert hall? They were not of the human race, for they left no trace of their presence. Was it possible that they were beings who had once been of this world, but no longer were? If so, what reason did they have for returning to the theatre? The only answer I can give you, my friend, is to come with me, for they are what this story is all about.

L ATE ONE NIGHT, as a light snow fell over all of Paris, a boy slowly crept towards the theatre. Finally, he had made it; he was away from that orphanage he had so long called a home—an orphanage that should never have been his home. True, his parents had died when he was just three years old, but he wasn't the only surviving member of his family. Somewhere in Paris, he knew, his grandfather was still alive. He didn't know where in Paris his grandfather was, or even what his grandfather's name was, but he knew that his grandfather could give him the loving home he had never had. He just had to find him first. And while he was searching, he would need to make sure the orphanage people couldn't find him.

The old, abandoned theatre would make the perfect hideout.

With a quick glance over his shoulder, the boy slipped inside through a broken window. There, he found himself standing in front of two large, charred, heavy wooden doors. As he pushed them open, they creaked loudly. The boy looked around the huge room that he had just entered. It appeared that it had once been the concert hall of the theatre, and it looked strangely familiar to him, but he didn't know why.

Well, he thought to himself, I guess this is home.

Suddenly, the hall was aglow with hundreds of candles, and music was coming from behind the curtain on the stage.

The boy was out the doors and through the window in a flash!

He tripped as he flew out the window, landing face-first in the snow. Breathing heavily, he stood up and brushed himself off.

What—or who—had been making that music? he wondered. Was it just his imagination? Could it have been... ghosts? The boy shivered at the thought.

No! his mind screamed at him. He would not be afraid. He, Gabriel Campeau, wouldn't let a bunch of musical ghosts scare him away. He escaped the cruelty of the orphanage, traveled all the way here to Paris; he was brave, smart...

And he had nowhere else to go.

The curtains in an apartment across the alley fluttered, and Gabriel quickly sneaked back into the theatre.

A middle-aged woman appeared on the apartment's balcony, her shadow stretching across the moonlit alley. Once again, music that sounded as if it were just outside her bedroom window had awakened her. It was so familiar, and it brought back many memories of her days spent in the theatre. She stared longingly at the theatre's faded walls. It had always held a special place in her heart, but even though it contained so many happy memories, the haunting memories of a night many years before kept her from ever reentering the theatre. If she had, she would have realized that the music she heard was much more than a dream.

ON THE OTHER side of the city, an elderly man tossed and turned from the nightmare that he had relived every night for the past ten years. It was so vivid; there he was, bowing as he was introduced to the biggest audience for whom he had ever performed. He turned around, and his wonderful orchestra began playing. Just as the song was ending, a blood-curdling scream came from somewhere backstage, and smoke poured into the concert hall. Panic and terror ensued as everyone attempted to escape the burning theatre. The most horrifying part of his nightmare was when he looked back into the theatre and saw people struggling to get out. People who were his friends, his co-workers, his family; people who, when the smoke had cleared, were gone.

The man wiped away a tear that slid down his face. Most of his orchestra had died in the fire, and the few who survived had left Paris soon after. He had gone from being the man in his dream, Alexandre Mierceles, the greatest conductor and composer in all of France, to nothing more than a frail old man with no friends, no family, and hardly anything left that was worth living for. His only daughter and her husband had perished on that tragic night, and their young son disappeared in all of the chaos. All he had left was his music, but he feared that that, too, would soon be nothing more than a memory.

FOR THE NEXT few days, Gabriel adjusted to his new, independent life. During the day, he would wander the streets, looking for someone kind enough to feed him. He also searched for a job, but this was challenging; not many people were interested in hiring a thirteen-year-old boy.

At night, Gabriel explored his hideout, everywhere from the box seats to the burned-out dressing rooms. In an office-type room, which had somehow survived the fire, he found a desk whose drawers were filled with scores of music! Each one was composed by a man named Alexandre Mierceles. At the very bottom of one of the drawers, Gabriel found an old, tattered photograph of a man and what appeared to be his daughter. The girl, who Gabriel guessed was about his age, looked, oddly enough, much like himself! Same dark, curly hair, same small, rounded nose, even similar elf-like ears. The only difference he could find was the eyes. While the girl's were big, round, and gentle, Gabriel had a mischievous gleam in his sharp, narrow eyes. Looking at the composer in the photograph, Gabriel saw that he, too, had that look. On the back of it, written in small, fancy letters, were the words "Alexandre and Jeanette Mierceles, Paris, France, 1908."

Gabriel's heart skipped a beat. His mother's name had been Jeanette, and he knew that she had been a violinist in the most famous orchestra in all of Paris. There was no doubt about it.

His grandfather was the famous Alexandre Mierceles!

"But where is he?" Gabriel asked himself. "Well, a famous composer can't be too hard to find. I'll start searching first thing in the morning!"

Gabriel was extremely excited to have discovered his grandfather's identity. A composer! And not just any composer, but the most renowned composer in all of Paris! All of France! All of Europe!

However, he would have to contain his excitement until tomorrow. Now, he had a concert to attend.

Gabriel curled up in the chair he used for a makeshift bed, notebook and pen in hand. All he had to do now was wait.

Every night, Gabriel spent some time writing music. He wrote for every instrument from the cello and bass to the piccolo and trumpet. He composed piece after piece, and after he finished for the night, he would blow out his candle, say his prayers, and listen as the mysterious orchestra began its performance. Some songs he recognized, and some he couldn't quite place, but they seemed very familiar, as if he had heard them long, long ago.

Tonight, though, he was tired, and he fell asleep as the ghosts played lullabies all around him.

WHILE READING the newspaper in his favorite café one morning, Alexandre Mierceles spied a headline that intrigued him:

Ghostly Happenings in Local Theatre

Neighbors of the once popular Leroux Theatre have rumored that ghosts are current inhabitants of the theatre. They have reported seeing lights flashing on and off inside the building, shadows of human figures moving around late at night, and the most mysterious of all: music of an entire symphony orchestra being played for half the night. One neighbor, Madame Loretta LaGue, said in an interview that she recognized a large amount of the music as that of composer and former conductor of the Leroux Theatre Orchestra, Alexandre Mierceles. No one has yet entered the theatre to verify or disprove the rumors, but Mme. LaGue says that she "will not tolerate this disturbance much longer, and if it continues, I will take action in discovering its cause by all means."

Mme. Loretta LaGue was a performer with the theatre before it closed.

"My word!" Alexandre cried. "Ghosts in the theatre, and little Loretta calling my music a disturbance? What is this world coming to?" A smile slowly crept over his face.

"Why, I haven't seen Loretta in over ten years!" he said to himself. "I think I'll arrange to meet with her. Then we can figure out what all this ghost business is about."

A mischievous gleam that had been absent for quite some time came into his eyes. He smiled again, then went back to his newspaper.

ALEXANDRE MIERCELES wasn't the only one who saw the article. Gabriel Campeau read the article, too, and he became worried. He figured that he would have to be on the lookout at all times in case someone did decide to investigate. Whatever happened, he could not let anyone find him, for fear they would send him back to the orphanage.

That wasn't the only part of the article that caught his eye. It also said that Mme. LaGue once performed in the theatre, and that she lived nearby.

"I'll bet she'll know where my grandfather is!" Gabriel said to himself. He made his decision: the next day, he would find Mme. LaGue and come one step closer to finding his grandfather!

As Gabriel waited for the orchestra to begin playing that night, he realized something: he hadn't yet looked behind the curtain; he had just assumed that the music was being played by ghosts. Gabriel's mom had been the lead violinist in the orchestra, and if the musicians really were visible ghosts... Gabriel took a deep breath... he would be able to see his mother again!

So when the orchestra began, Gabriel walked onto the stage and poked his head behind the curtain. Disappointment met him. The instruments were all being played, but the beings that played them were invisible. Despite this fact, he still felt a special warmth and comfort, a tranquility he had never felt before, in knowing that the violin that was hovering over the first chair was being played by his mother.

Gabriel finished listening to the performance, then sank into a peaceful sleep.

LORETTA LAGUE anxiously waited at the window of her apartment, excited and nervous about the famous conductor's visit. It had been so long since they had last seen one another, and he had been like a father to her during her days in the theatre.

She predicted that his time in her home would be bittersweet; it would be great for them to see each other and reminisce about "the good old days," but discussion of the fire was imminent. After all, the main purpose of the visit was for him to find out more about the "ghosts." Loretta felt sorry for him because, while she had lost only her job after the fire, his most prized possession, his daughter, Jeanette, had been taken from him. He probably hoped that Jeanette was one of the ghosts, and that he would be able to see and talk to her again.

Loretta sighed. There were no ghosts, she strongly believed. She hated to think of Alexandre's disappointment on discovering that, but it was the truth, and he would have to face it. All of her neighbors had spread those rumors, but she knew that there was some logical explanation for it.

There was a knock at the door.

"That will be Monsieur Mierceles himself," she said, and after a quick glance in the mirror, she went to greet her caller.

Much to her surprise, however, the person at her door was not the composer but a young, shabby boy. You and I know him as Gabriel, but Mme. Loretta LaGue had not yet met him, so she looked on him in disgust.

"Can you not see, boy, that this is the home of a proper lady and not a place that welcomes beggars?" she snapped when she saw Gabriel at her door.

"Madame LaGue," he calmly replied. "I have not come to beg; I only want to know if you have any information on how I might contact Monsieur Alexandre Mierceles."

"Why?" she asked suspiciously.

Gabriel hesitated, but then answered, "He is my grandfather."

A look of shock spread over Mme. LaGue's face.

"He is to arrive at any minute," she stammered. "Won't you come in?" she added nervously.

Alexandre Mierceles came very soon.

"Oh, Loretta, it's so good to see you again!" he exclaimed upon his arrival. After greeting each other with a hug and a kiss to both cheeks, they walked into the parlor, where Gabriel was waiting.

The old composer froze the moment he entered the room. His eyes met with Gabriel's.

Impossible! was Alexandre's first thought.

I knew it! was Gabriel's.

He has everything like her: same nose, same hair, same mouth, everything! Alexandre's mind was racing.

In a stunned silence, they walked slowly towards each other. Overjoyed, Alexandre embraced Gabriel, and their eyes—their sharp, mischievous eyes—began filling with tears, and soon everyone in the room was crying.

"Gabriel," Alexandre whispered, "Gabriel!"

And Gabriel's lips formed the word of a long-forgotten memory. "Grandfather."

Eight Months Later

Conductors and Composers
M. Alexandre Mierceles and
M. Gabriel Campeau
present
The Leroux Theatre Orchestra

After eleven years, they have finally
returned to give us what was meant to be the most
spectacular performance
of their time.
Please join us on
Saturday, September 22, 1935
for this masterpiece concert.

IT HAD TAKEN eight months of long, hard work, but the theatre had finally been restored to its former glory. Now, conductor and grandson stood onstage, batons in hand, with both of their music ready to be performed.

The theatre was just as it had been eleven years before; the bright chandelier, red velvet seats, a new curtain, and an extremely large audience. Only this time, it was even better. Now, there were two composers, two conductors, and two people who agreed that they were the happiest people in the world.

With the help of Loretta, they had managed to find most of the surviving orchestra members, and many children of former musicians had returned to play as well.

The Mierceleses had formed a whole new orchestra, and they were determined to give the best performance of the century.

The lights dimmed, and as it had at the beginning of this story and on that dreadful night so many years before, the audience heard the soft, sweet sound of a violin, not played by Gabriel's mother, but by Gabriel himself! The violin was soon joined by the entire orchestra, and it was the most spectacular performance Paris had ever heard!

So THERE YOU have it, my friend. You have discovered who the mysterious performers were and seen many lives changed along the way. It was the ghosts of the orchestra that had called Gabriel towards the theatre when he had nowhere to go. They played not only because they wanted to give the performance they never gave, but because they wanted Gabriel to feel at peace while he hid from the world and searched for his grandfather. They wanted him to be comforted by their music. If the orchestra hadn't begun to play, Alexandre Mierceles would never have read the newspaper article, Mme. LaGue would never have given the interview, and who knows how long Gabriel would have spent searching for his grandfather.

So you see, the ghosts were not only behind the curtain of the theatre, but behind everything wonderful that happened in this story: Gabriel feeling safe in the theatre and having the chance to compose music that was almost, if not just as good as his grandfather's. And Gabriel was given a home, a home with family, a home with love, and a home filled with music.

Bats and Pearls

by Cara Kornhaus, age 13

RAINDROPS FELL from the dark velvety sky, dropping delicately onto the world below. A few clouds drifted through the gloom, covering the moon and few stars that had escaped the light of the city that flourished down the river.

Five fruit bats glided through the air, each trying to find enough food for themselves before the rain started to pour down. The only reason they were staying together was that, if one bat found any sign of food, he wouldn't be able to get it all for himself.

Four of the five bats flapped a considerably long distance from the last one. They were bigger, with longer wings to allow them to fly farther and faster. They flew out every night to look for food, and they were veterans at it.

The fifth bat was a young creature called Seed. This was his first time venturing out of the cave where he was born. He had been smart enough to go with the most skilled fliers to search for food, but he was quickly tiring. His wings felt like lead. He bit his

Cara was living in San Antonio, Texas, when her story appeared in the January/February 2009 issue of Stone Soup.

THE STONE SOUP BOOK

tongue, struggling to keep up with the others, but he was much smaller than any of them.

"Hey, wait up!" he gasped. The other bats didn't pay any attention. The rain came down harder. A bolt of lightning shot through the air, and a crack of thunder followed quickly after. The older bats dived, but Seed couldn't tell where they had gone. "I can't fly!" he cried, his wet wings flapping uselessly. He tumbled from the sky, down toward the ground. The world snapped out of view, and numbness spread through him. He was unconscious before he could cry out.

A MUSKRAT SAT on her haunches at the edge of the river, carefully scrubbing the spherical pearl in her paws of any dirt. She didn't mind the rain pelting down onto her fur. She kind of liked it, actually. Not like that silly duck that sat hunched up in her nest as if the rain would burn her. The muskrat smiled as she lifted the pearl and watched it sparkle, evidently as clean as it would get. She was just about to turn and go back to her lodge when something caught her eye.

A dark shape floated toward her. She stood on her hind legs to get a better look at it. It was definitely a creature of some sort, but she couldn't tell what kind it was. She waded into the river, the current rushing past her faster than it usually went because of all the rain. The strange creature wasn't moving—it was either dead or unconscious. The muskrat seized the animal around the middle with her paws and hauled him to shore. She was enthralled with how this creature looked. It had long, thin membranes stretched across its forelegs, which she guessed served as wings. The bat stirred and coughed. He opened his eyes and stared around at the river. The muskrat gently lifted him into her lodge, which was made of grass, sticks, and dried mud.

"Who are you?" the bat asked suspiciously. He wiped his eyes with his thumbs.

"Me? Oh, I'm Azure," the muskrat said cheerfully. She looked curiously at the bat. "You're a bat, aren't you? How'd you get in the river?" The bat ignored her. She shook her head and stashed the pearl, which she realized she was still holding, behind a pile of sticks.

"What was that?" the bat demanded.

"Nothing," Azure replied. "I'm going to catch some fish!" She left rather quickly. The bat stood on his feet and looked around. The inside of the lodge was completely empty of anything of interest, except perhaps the thing that Azure had stashed away. He decided he would investigate that later.

"Hey, Bat, have you ever tried fish?" Azure asked, crawling back into the lodge with two pink fish wriggling in her paws.

"My name is Seed!" the bat protested. "And I only eat fruit!" He lifted his right wing and licked it, attempting to get it dry.

"You're not even going to thank me for saving your life?" the muskrat asked, appalled. Seed ignored her once more. He stretched and yawned widely, then climbed to the ceiling of the lodge and hung upside down, immediately drifting into dreams filled with apples and pears. Azure curled into a ball and fell asleep as well, planning to teach the little bat some manners in the morning.

SEED'S FEET SLIPPED. He landed on the ground with a bump, waking instantly. Fuming, he rubbed his furry head and crept to the entrance of the muskrat lodge. It had stopped raining, and the sun was high in the sky. The bat shielded his sensitive eyes. Azure was paddling skillfully through the water, clutching a fish in her mouth. Seed glared at her. More fish! Why didn't she go get him some fruit? He turned and went back inside, his stomach growling. The sunlight was hurting his eyes, and he liked the darkness of the lodge much better. He was about to climb back onto the ceiling when he remembered. What had the muskrat hidden? He reached behind the sticks where she had put it, and to his amazement he drew out a snow-white pearl. Seed grasped it in his wing tip and marveled at it. If he brought this back with him to his cave, maybe the others would be so impressed that they wouldn't leave him alone in the rain the next time they left to find food!

He couldn't dwell on this thought very long, though, because at that moment a gunshot rang out, startling him so much that he dropped the pearl. There was a scuffling from outside, and Azure crawled into her lodge, out of breath and with wide eyes.

"A hunter!" she gasped. She hurried to the far corner of her lodge and crouched there. "Stay in here." Seed bit his lip. He wanted to stay out of the hunter's way, but what better chance did he have of making it out of Azure's home with the pearl? Cradling the beautiful thing in his wing tip, he stepped to the entrance and sneered at the muskrat.

"Do you think the other bats will like this?" he asked, displaying the pearl. Azure opened her mouth, closed it, then turned her stunned look into a ferocious scowl.

"Give it to me," she said menacingly. Seed's heart quivered with fear, but the sneer sat frozen on his face.

"I don't think I should give it to you. I mean, you have no real use for it. And the bats back home will love me for this!" Seed snickered. "You could try to follow me, I guess. But... oh, yeah! Isn't muskrat fur valuable to hunters?" Azure lunged at the bat, but he was flying away from the lodge before she could blink.

"I saved your life, you vile creature!" she screamed. "I trusted you!" Seed felt a pang of guilt. How strange—he had never felt it before. With the pearl stashed safely in his mouth, he alighted upside down on a tree branch and watched the lodge to see how Azure was taking this defeat.

She wasn't in the lodge.

"THAT PEARL WAS given to one of my ancestors by a sea rat he rescued!" the muskrat snarled as she made her way across the river, heading straight for Seed's tree. "It was passed down generation to generation!" Seed was so surprised by her actions that he let go of the branch, only barely managing to catch hold of the next one down. He began to get frantic. Was she crazy? She was going to get herself killed! But wait, no. There were no hunters near this area. Satisfied, Seed dropped from the tree and took wing in the other direction.

Blam! Blam! The gunshots rang through the forest. The bat let out a startled cry and lost height, checking every part of him to make sure he wasn't hit. It took him a second to register the blood in the water.

"Azure!" The cry was horrible. She lay motionless, carried away by the current of the river. The hunter's dogs were already going after her, barking excitedly. The bat lost all altitude and tumbled to the ground, breathing heavily. "No... no..." he moaned. She was dead. His only friend in the world. Dead! The word spun through his head, making him dizzy with horror and fear.

The dogs sloshed through the water, bending down and grasping Azure's limp body in their mouths. The hunter whistled to them, loading his gun for his next kill. Anger suddenly surged through the bat's body. That human was just standing there! He had just killed an innocent creature and he was just standing there!

"You leave her alone!" Seed found himself shrieking, once again in the air. The pearl still sat lodged in his mouth, interfering with his speech. So it was really just a bunch of jumbled syllables that not even he could understand. Seed flew straight for the hunter's face.

If you've ever had an angry bat streaking straight toward you, you know it's a bit unnerving. The hunter stepped back, raising his gun toward the bat. He was about to pull the trigger when he saw that the creature held a pearl in its mouth.

"What the...?" the man said in confusion. He was surprised enough to let down his guard for a split second. That was all that Seed needed. The little bat flapped right up to the man, buffeting him with his wings.

"Eek! Eeaaaccchh! Rahacch!" Seed cried, not sure what he was saying. The pearl dropped from his mouth, and the man lost no time in snatching it from the ground. In two seconds he was off and running, not caring about his newest muskrat prize. He just wanted to be sure he didn't get rabies from the crazy bat.

SEED COLLAPSED to the ground, moaning. He buried his head in his wings and sobbed. If he hadn't stolen the pearl, then the muskrat wouldn't have chased him, and she wouldn't be dead... She had been so nice, catching food for him and letting him stay in her home! Why on earth had he been so ungrateful?!

"Don't cry so hard. If you do, you'll get dehydrated. And the dumbest place to get dehydrated is by the river." Seed whipped around, his eyes wide in astonishment. Azure crawled onto the bank, her face twisted in pain.

"A-Azure! How! How did you..." he trailed off, just stood in amazement.

"His aim was off," she replied, trying to hide her pain. "He got me in the leg. But those dogs... those horrible dogs didn't care whether I was dead or alive, they just grabbed me..." she shuddered. Seed looked down at the ground, guilt replacing his sadness.

"Azure... I'm so sorry. I... I was just selfish. And I lost your pearl." He began to cry again. The muskrat nodded solemnly.

"I guess I was unfair to you, too. If I hadn't hidden the pearl like it was some big deal, you wouldn't have stolen it, right?"

"Probably not," Seed muttered. He sighed. "Azure, I can't go back home. At the cave we don't really believe in helping each other and... we're just so selfish." He shifted uncomfortably as he said this. "So... I was hoping I could stay at the river. I could find my own home and everything!" Azure stared into his eyes, but the cold, hardened look that had previously been there was gone. In its place now stood sincere hope. The muskrat nodded.

"Of course you can stay, Seed," she said quietly. "I know of some fruit trees down the river." She smiled, and the bat smiled back. Right then, there was no place he would rather be. No place other than with his best friend.

The Journey Begins

by Anna Hirtes, age 9

Stories of the Unicorns
Book One

When God created the earth, he asked Adam in the Garden of Eden to name the animals. When Adam picked the unicorn to name first, God reached down and touched the unicorn's horn. This is a sign that unicorns are blessed above all other creatures.

—Nancy Hathaway, The Unicorn

SHELLY LOOKED LONGINGLY at the big jugs of water being sold in the shops scattered along the dusty street.

"Hey, hey, hey, girlie! Get off the road! You're blocking it with your over-large body!" The voice laughed heartily. Shelly sighed. They were the rich boys and newspaper boys. Their favorite activity was to tease Shelly. They were trying to provoke her to come and hit them. Then Shelly would be arrested and severely punished by the government.

Anna was living in Basking Ridge, New Jersey, when her story appeared in the September/October 2007 issue of Stone Soup.

THE STONE SOUP BOOK

Shelly flicked her long, red wavy hair out of her face. It fell far past her waist, and many folks thought it greatly needed cutting. Her big green eyes swept the street, searching constantly for dropped or forgotten coins. The nine-year-old girl pushed her small body through the crowds. She desperately wished it was Christmas, her birthday. It was the only day of the year when she allowed herself to buy a feast.

The boys were partly right about her. Shelly was a beggar girl and was extremely scarce of money.

The cold evening wind blew her dress and hair. Shelly could see her wispy clouds of breath and decided to head back to her alleyway. When she at last reached her beloved alley, Shelly immediately curled up in her few blankets. One of them had been hers ever since she could remember. It was silvery blue with a single unicorn embroidered in the middle. The thick blanket felt a thousand times better than silk. Shelly wouldn't, couldn't ever part with it.

Shelly wrapped herself in that special possession and the other thin brown sheets she owned. Her box stood overhead, weather-beaten and dirty. It was so large, Shelly was sure it once held a bed frame. An eventful sleep took over Shelly.

First she dreamed she was walking in a field of unicorns. The earth turned blacker than black and colder than cold. A black-hooded figure loomed toward Shelly through the magnificently never-ending darkness. Shelly backed away and tripped over her own unsteady feet. The figure of darkness (at least that's what Shelly thought it was) gracefully curved its body downward toward Shelly's face. At that precise moment, the dreaming girl woke up, breathing hard and sweating. "It was just a dream," she told herself firmly, "just an old dream. It's not hurting anyone, and it's not real." Shelly tried to sound confident, but her voice trembled slightly.

"Big sign of madness, talking to your own head," stated a newspaper boy by the name of Frederick Afintger, who was passing. He smirked. Shelly ignored him.

Dawn was Shelly's favorite time of day. Most people were still snug in bed. No one shot insults at her, she was free of owners of stalls and shops shouting at her to get away from their selling areas. Shelly was sick of that. Now the girl grabbed the last of her bread loaf and headed for the stream.

It was warm, especially for this time of day. Shelly finally reached the cold, playful stream that flowed around the edge of the enchanted place, Magic Forest. The beggar girl took a long, refreshing drink from the creek. When Shelly finished munching on her bread loaf, she waded into the water. The deepest place reached up to her knees. Shelly stared absentmindedly at the horizon. The sun was still determined to climb over the mountain. The sun had almost accomplished that goal, which it repeated every morning. Shelly marched back to the bank and dried herself off. Suddenly, she glimpsed a flash of white in the trees. Shelly started. Then she saw it again, farther away this time.

"Hello?" Shelly called out. "Anybody there?" No answer. Shelly entered the Magic Forest and sprinted toward the white. She ran until she could run no more. A stitch had arisen in Shelly's side and her breathing was fast and hard.

She had arrived in a clearing. A small, lush apple tree stood in the corner, its fruits swaying slightly in the breeze. The very same creek Shelly had earlier waded in flowed before her. The stream opened into a little pool. Curiously, it was silvery. It must come from here and go around the wood, Shelly thought to herself. Shelly sighed heavily for no particular reason and headed for the apple tree.

She heard a hiss and tripped over a tree root, or she thought it was a tree root. Fangs sank into her leg and poison shot through her body. Hooves pounding like thunder, and everything went black.

Everything was blurry and Shelly could hear a faint neighing sound. With difficulty, she sat up and slowly looked around. There, trotting along the path toward her, was a unicorn!

THE STONE SOUP BOOK

He had a long, flowing, milky-white mane, tail, and fore-lock. His eyes were like crystals, glowing in the bright sunlight. His hooves were cloven like a goat, and the fur was silky. It was beautifully white. He came over to her. Shelly didn't know how to feel. The unicorn started to speak in a strange language. Oddly, Shelly could understand it.

"Hello, my name is Magic Star. What is your name?" the unicorn asked.

Shelly replied shakily, "My name is Shelly. I am an orphan." For a moment, Shelly thought she saw an excited look on Magic Star's face. But when she blinked, it was once again replaced by a curious expression.

"What happened to me? Are you really a unicorn? Why are you here? Where are we? Was that a snake? If it was, did you kill it? Do you live here? Is this forest dangerous? Why is that pool silvery...?" It all came pouring out before Shelly could stop herself.

"Slow down, slow down! I can't possibly answer all those questions at once!" Magic Star exclaimed. "I will answer each one the best I can. I am a real unicorn and that was a snake that attacked you. A rattlesnake. I did not kill it. I terrified it so it would stay away from you. This place is called the Unicorn Clearing, in the heart of Magic Forest. I stay here sometimes. This forest can be dangerous at times, but you are safe with me. That pool is silvery because it is a unicorn pool. I am here because I sensed danger. Does that answer all of your questions?"

Shelly nodded. She tried to stand, but she collapsed back down at the pain in her leg.

"Does it hurt?" Magic Star asked.

"Very much," Shelly replied.

"Then I will heal it," Magic Star told Shelly, lowering his horn toward the snakebite. Before Shelly could say a word, the bite was gone.

"Thank you!" said Shelly gratefully. Suddenly, they heard hoofbeats loud and close.

"On my back!" Magic Star demanded. He quickly sunk down on his knees and Shelly scrambled on the silky white back. Magic Star leapt easily over the unicorn pool and bolted into the depths of the Magic Forest. After what seemed like hours, the breathless unicorn stopped.

Shelly dismounted and looked around. They had arrived in another clearing, except there were berry bushes here and no pool, only a lively little stream. Shelly turned back to Magic Star. She opened her mouth to speak, but Magic Star started first.

"That was the king's men. They are after me." Shelly once again nodded. Magic Star continued, "It is not very safe for me here, but luckily I am faster than their horses." He looked around the clearing, as if expecting the king's men to jump out of the trees and ambush at any moment.

Suddenly, Magic Star dashed into a standing position. Shelly had heard a rustle in the forest and supposed Magic Star must have, too.

"Get behind me!" Magic Star stated.

"No, wait," Shelly replied firmly. The unicorn gave her an annoyed look, but she ignored it. Shelly continued to move cautiously toward the trees. She passed a big brown oak tree.

Shelly looked on the other side, and her mouth fell open in shock. There, standing before her, was a girl. And she wasn't just any girl. Shelly and she were identical. They both had those big green eyes, long red wavy hair, and everything else. The two girls were even built the same. No difference in their appearance was visible.

"Who are you?" they said in unison. Both smiled in spite of themselves.

"My name is Shelly," Shelly answered.

The mysterious girl responded, "My name is Elizabeth. I'm very pleased to meet you, Shelly." She held out a hand identical to Shelly's.

"I am pleased to meet you too, Elizabeth," Shelly replied, taking the hand and shaking it. At that moment, Magic Star happened to come into the forest where they were.

"There you are..." He stopped in midsentence at the sight of Elizabeth. "Oh, great," he said sarcastically under his breath. "This wasn't the plan!"

Elizabeth asked, "What did you say?" She tried to hide her pleasure at meeting a unicorn, but was doing a very poor job of it.

"Nothing," Magic Star answered sheepishly. Elizabeth shrugged and started toward the clearing.

When she saw no one was coming with her, she turned around and said, "Well, are you coming?" Shelly and Magic Star followed the lively Elizabeth. Elizabeth started humming a tune. Girl and unicorn headed back to the clearing together. Reader, this is how the great journey began.

Flynn

by Hugh Cole, age 11

FLYNN CADARA LOOKED up at the sky. It was getting dark. He knew that he needed to head back to the cabin. It would be dinnertime undeniably, and he didn't want to miss it.

"Tam!" Flynn called out.

A large, wolflike dog appeared, heading toward Flynn at a slow trot.

"It's time to head home," Flynn said. "Did you find anything interesting?"

"There's a large herd of elk not far from here," Tam said to him, looking up at Flynn's face as they headed up a low hill. "You should tell your father. Winter is coming, and he hasn't been able to get much meat."

"I'll tell him."

"Also, bear tracks," said the burly dog.

"Agh, blast and confound it all! Why bears!"

"Just tell the bear to stay away from the sheep and the horses," Tam said, unconcerned.

Hugh was living in Moscow, Idaho, when his story appeared in the November/December 2008 issue of Stone Soup.

TALLINN CADARA, Flynn's father, peered into the darkness from the porch of a small cabin. He saw Flynn come out of the dark and into the warm glow that the oil lantern was casting. The boy was tall for his age, ten, and was skinny and lanky. He was wearing tough britches cut just below the kneecaps, and a short-sleeved shirt, and no shoes. His hair was a gray-brown color, and his face's details were sharp.

"What took you so long, son! And what have I told you about those, those... pants! Winter's not a month away! And you don't even have your boots on!" Tallinn called out in frustration.

"My boots are too small, and these pants are more comfortable!"

"Oh, well, we'll go into town tomorrow to get you some more boots, but if you wear those, those... shorts anymore before winter is over, I'll burn them. Come inside, we're having supper. Your mother is worried sick about you."

Tallinn was a strong man, a kind but firm father. Flynn understood that he didn't want him to get pneumonia or anything, but his "shorts," as Tallinn had called them, were much more comfortable, and his legs didn't get hot or stuffy.

Flynn came inside and approached his mother, Selenia. She was setting the table with stew and bread and pale cider. When she saw Flynn come in, she crossed her arms and gave him a large scowl.

"I have a mind to not let you eat, young man," she said in a voice shaking with concern. She hugged Flynn and sat him down at the table. Tallinn came in and sat down. Selenia said the grace, and they all began to eat. Flynn had worked up an appetite, and he ate large portions of food. Tam, who had found his bowl, was tearing at the slab of meat ravenously.

"Did you see anything interesting or important today?" asked Selenia, to see if Flynn had an excuse for being so late.

"Yes. There's a large herd of elk, not far from here," he said, slurping up a spoonful of the stew.

That seemed to redeem Flynn to his father, who was grinning

widely. "Get the bows ready, and we'll head out tonight!"

A spark shot through Flynn. They were going to go hunting! This meant that they could go farther than he was normally allowed, so he would be able to explore more. What's more, they were going at night. He felt bad, though, for the elk, as they would be killed.

"No, you won't leave tonight," Selenia broke in, "at least not until my son has had some sleep."

"Selenia! I don't nee-" protested Flynn.

"Don't you argue with me, young man. You're not going hunting until morning, and that's that."

Flynn knew that he had lost the argument, short as it was. He went to his small bed in one of the corners of the two-room cabin. He pulled off his clothes and crawled under the warm blankets. He thought about all of the familiar territory he had crept through that day, all of the birds and squirrels he had chatted with. He thought about his strange ability to talk with animals, something that he had not shared with Tallinn or Selenia. He pondered this subject for a long while before he fell asleep.

FLYNN JERKED UP in the middle of the night. He hadn't told Tallinn about the bear, and he hadn't yet had a chance to talk to him. The sheep! He dashed up, pulled on his clothes, and dashed to Tallinn's bed, which was across the room from his. Selenia was slumbering fitfully, but... Tallinn wasn't in the bed. Flynn looked over at Tam's small bed. Empty too.

"Come on, are you coming or not!" whispered a voice below him, making him jump. It was Tam.

"What?" Flynn whispered back.

"We have to get to the elk as soon as possible. We won't have this chance every day. C'mon!"

"Selenia said..." Flynn began.

"Don't pretend that you don't want to go hunting, Flynn. I'm sure Selenia will understand when she has meat for the winter."

Convinced, Flynn hurriedly put on several layers of clothes and rummaged under his bed for his old, small pair of boots. He grabbed his wool cap and then followed Tam outside, where his father was waiting.

"Ready to go?" asked Tallinn, rubbing wax along the string of his long hunting bow.

"Yes."

"Good."

They headed out into the thick woods as silently as possible, Tam trotting ahead, showing Flynn the way to the elk.

They made good progress, speeding through the woods. Flynn couldn't bring himself to tell Tallinn about the bear, for his father would undoubtedly kill it when he most certainly did not need to. All Flynn could do was hope that they came across the bear before it killed any sheep.

"Flynn! Up ahead!" Tam barked.

"This is where the elk were," Flynn told Tallinn, pointing ahead.

"Now we must go slowly and silently. If the elk are still there, then they'll hear us if we're not careful. You stay here, and I'll scout ahead." Tallinn crept forward through the forest and down into the steep valley. Flynn stayed where he was, and then he heard a huge roar. A roar that couldn't be the bear.

Flynn heard his father yelp and Tam scream his challenge to whatever was down there. Flynn dashed forward and gazed down.

Tallinn was loosing arrows at a huge monster. Tam was dashing in at it, biting and tearing at its legs. Flynn squinted down at the beast, trying to figure what it was, but he couldn't.

It looked like a bear, though much larger. It roared out into the night and looked over, directly into Flynn's eyes. A huge, fiery pain shot through Flynn like an arrow. He felt dizzy and fell to the ground. The shapes of Tallinn and Tam and the thing below him grew to shadows and shades, and then Flynn's mind went blank, and he fell, unconscious.

FLYNN WAS ROUSED back into consciousness by the cracking of trees being mowed over by the wailing beast. It was crashing off through the forest.

Flynn stood up gingerly and slowly walked down to Tallinn, who was panting, crouching next to Tam. The big dog was gasping in ragged breaths. Tallinn stood up.

"What was that!" Flynn gasped.

"I don't know," Tallinn said, but Flynn wondered if he really did.

"What made it run away?" Flynn asked Tam quietly as they walked back to the cabin.

"Your father hit it in the eye."

"How did he know to do that?" Flynn inquired, but they were back at the cabin. Tallinn and Flynn slowly crept in, took off their clothes, and got into bed, trying not to disturb Selenia.

THE NEXT MORNING, Flynn got up and asked his father if he could go out.

Tallinn said no.

Flynn understood, but he still needed to find the bear. So he went out while his father was chopping wood behind the house.

Neither of them had spoken a word of the last night's incident to Selenia, and for good reason. While Flynn searched for the bear, he thought about the huge monster. And then a huge idea hit him like a thunderbolt. Why hadn't he tried to talk to the thing! Probably because he was glued to the spot, petrified, but he should have tried.

When Flynn found the bear, a huge grizzly, he talked to it for a while, asking it about the monster. The bear said that he didn't know anything about a phantom beast. Finally Flynn asked him to leave the sheep alone, though he told him about the elk, which seemed to interest the bear greatly.

WHEN FLYNN GOT home, relieved that Tallinn didn't find out about his outing, he went inside. That night, Tallinn called Flynn out to the porch of the cabin.

"Don't ask me any questions, Flynn, just listen," said Tallinn. "What we saw last night was an Alarcon. One on a mission. No, don't ask any questions," Tallinn repeated, seeing that Flynn was about to speak. "I think I know what its mission is," Tallinn continued.

"What?"

"To capture you, and use your powers."

Flynn couldn't believe his father's answer. "What?"

"You can talk to animals, can't you, son?"

"How did you know?" asked Flynn in alarm.

"I see you continually conversing with Tam, in a way that couldn't be just friendly dog-talk. And I know that you are special. If the Alarcon comes back looking for you, you're going to have to leave."

"What?" Flynn asked confusedly.

"Eventually, it will get to you, and I don't want to let that happen—will not let that happen. You will flee, with Tam, and get as far away as you can. I'm pretty sure that Tam knows of a good place to take you. Though you must go, without arguing."

Without waiting for Flynn to reply, Tallinn began to push him into the house.

"Wait, Tallinn, what about Selenia?" Flynn asked.

"I will talk to your mother."

"One more thing."

"What?"

"How did you know about the monster?"

Tallinn hesitated. "Ask Tam to tell you, and I'm sure he will."

"OK," Flynn said, and he went and got into his bed.

OVER THE NEXT few weeks, Flynn rarely went out. He constantly asked Tam about the monster whenever Selenia was out of sight, though the big dog refused to give any details. He continuously told Flynn that he would tell him when the time was right, though Tam didn't say when the time would be.

Tallinn told Selenia about the entire ordeal, which of course made her very angry. Just before she was about to burst, they all heard a wail, and then a roar, that sounded awfully familiar.

They all stood for a split second and then snapped into action.

Tam dashed outside to keep watch, while Tallinn urgently gave Flynn instructions. "Follow Tam. Stay with him, and heed his commands. He will keep you safe. Don't look back. Your mother has a pack ready for you. Go!" Tallinn then rushed for his bow and ran outside.

Flynn rushed into the hands of Selenia, and she pressed a kiss onto the top of his head. She handed him a sack of food and gear. "Forgive your father for that rough farewell, though he wants you safe. Be safe, be brave, and be wise. Good luck. I love you," she said.

Tears pouring out of his eyes, Flynn followed Tam out of the back door, and, just as the cabin was out of sight, Flynn heard the wail of the beast.

Tam ran Flynn hard for several hours after the wailing of the beast was out of earshot. The dog wanted to keep going, but Flynn insisted that he needed a rest. Tam gave him a few minutes.

Flynn sat down with his back to a tree and dug into his sack. He saw a small knife, lots of food, a canteen of water, a little bottle of medicine, and some extra clothing. He pulled out a chunk of cheese and got a slice of bread. He devoured them hungrily and then took a short nap.

Tam woke him up after he too had had food, a small porcupine. He didn't make Flynn run, but rather walk quickly.

Then the dog, rather suddenly, began to talk. "Now, Flynn, the time is right. The thing that you saw, and is most likely chasing us, is called an Alarcon."

"I know already. Tallinn told me a little about it, though keep going," Flynn said, anxious to understand the Alarcon completely.

"It's sensitive in the eyes, and it's the fiercest, most brutal, most savage beast in the entire country. Somehow, it knows that you can speak to animals, and it clearly wants that ability. And it can get it. Its eyes are how it does it. If it looks you in the eye, it slowly drains you of your powers and takes them for itself."

Flynn remembered the pain that had pierced through his body when the Alarcon had looked him in the eyes.

"Explain my powers," Flynn asked.

"You have your ability because your great-great-grandfather didn't kill an animal when he was starving to death and when he had the opportunity. The animal granted him the power and then showed him food. That's all. And the power was passed down in your family," Tam said quickly and simply.

"Wait," asked Flynn, perplexed. "If it passes down in the family, why doesn't my father have the power?"

"It was on your mother's side, though she lost it when she married a man from a different country."

Flynn thought about the sacrifice his mother had made.

And then, cutting off the conversation, was the roar of the Alarcon. It was close. Very close. Too close.

A huge tree toppled not a foot away from where Flynn stood, thrown by the huge beast. It was right there, and uprooting another tree.

"Run!" Tam barked, and Flynn ran, the Alarcon following close behind the dog and the boy.

Flynn was soon tired, and the Alarcon was almost on top of him.

And then, Flynn fell, and Tam fell, and the Alarcon fell. They plummeted down, having run head-on off of a cliff.

Flynn gazed down, horror rising up in his chest. They were falling into a rock field. Huge, sharp, jutting rocks stuck up out of the earth, and they were not a hundred yards from the huge stones.

And then, a huge condor was under Tam, and Flynn, and shot back up to the edge of the cliff, leaving the Alarcon to burst apart on the crude rocks.

THE CONDOR FLEW back to the cabin, which was now in ruins. It appeared that the Alarcon had stepped on it, and more than half of it was crushed. Tallinn and Selenia were well, though quite upset about the cabin.

Flynn thanked the condor, who nodded and flew off.

Flynn ran into the arms of his parents.

The Tale of the Strange Nobleman

by Talitha Farschman, age 12

ONCE UPON A TIME, there lived a beautiful noble lady whose name was Thione. She was loved and cherished by all of her people, and her wisdom was prized for miles around. Her husband also was a brave and noble man, and loved by his people just as much as his wife. His name was Lord Paul, and he was lord over many of the king's provinces.

And so when the king invited him to a feast to celebrate his own marriage, Lord Paul had to attend, and his wife, Lady Thione, stayed to govern the castle during his absence.

The journey was hard, but after weeks of travel, Lord Paul and his retinue entered the king's palace. The feast was indeed as great as the king had said in his letter of invitation, and the splendor and aroma of the food made even the pickiest of the courtiers' mouths water.

There was fruit in abundance, meat stews, beef, pork, and chicken, a great variety of cheeses and breads, and wine that came specifically from the king's cellars in honor of his bride.

Talitha was living in Roseville, California, when her story appeared in the May/June 2008 issue of Stone Soup.

Yet happy as he was, Lord Paul also felt lonely for his fair Lady Thione, for he felt that the beauty of the new queen did not rival her, and soon this loneliness shown forth not only in his heart, but in his face, and the king, being keen of eye, noticed, and being slightly drunk from the overabundance of wine, was offended and inquired of his lord's woe.

"How can I be happy, O my king," Lord Paul answered, "when I long for my own wife whose wisdom is famed in the provinces and whose beauty goes unrivaled?"

Then the king was furious for he felt that his wife's beauty would surely surpass any who dared to boast in such a way. Therefore, he, in anger, had Lord Paul sent to the dungeons, until "the woman of whom he boasted should prove her wisdom to be greater than his queen's."

So he sent his decree to Lady Thione, convinced that nothing could rescue Lord Paul from his sentence.

YET, AS ALWAYS, Lady Thione thought wisely and devoted all of her time to thinking of a way to rescue her husband on the king's terms. Many days and nights she stayed in her tower, thinking and praying, till on the morning of the third day she emerged with a scheme. Quickly she commanded that a great and beautiful bow, inlaid with gold and silver, be made, along with a quiver of arrows of equal workmanship.

Then she called to the blacksmiths for gauntlets and leggings of mail to be made, along with an iron helmet. Then she and her maids set to work on the finest embroidered shirt and tunic that could be made out of fine silk and velvet, stitching in many patterns, making it as beautiful an attire as possible. For one entire month they worked, none knowing what she was scheming.

Finally, on the first day of spring, Lady Thione and her maids finished the strange-looking garment.

She arrayed herself with the heavily embroidered shirt and tunic, tying them in place with a green silk sash into which she thrust two foreign knives. Then she did up her hair and put on her helmet, along with the chain-mail leggings and gauntlets, and a few articles of gold, finally slinging on her bow and quiver.

In that strange array, she looked like a young formidable prince from a far land, and her presence struck awe into her servants' hearts. So she mounted her black mare and rode to the king's palace.

THE KING COULD make nothing of the lordly stranger, except that he must be a great prince from a faraway land. His display of wealth was either the rashness of a fool, or he did not fear that anything would be stolen. The king decided upon the latter when he recognized the youth's quiet, cold, yet courteous attitude.

So he politely invited the travel-stained lordling into his hall, and asked him why he had come.

The disguised Thione replied using a strange accent, "I have journeyed for many miles, as it is the custom of my country to learn of those who live beyond our great borders."

The king was unfazed. But his wife was a little more suspicious and, whispering to the king, said, "O my king, I would be wary of that one, for something in me says that that is no man, but a woman who lies beneath that barbarian apparel."

The king looked at the waiting prince and softly replied, "Perhaps, Queen, but I feel inclined to test this noble stranger before making such a judgment. If it would ease your heart, then I shall have you devise what three tests should be given him."

To this the queen agreed, and the king turned again to the foreign prince. "In honor of your stay, we shall hold a feast, and events appropriate shall be named, of which I hope you will partake." The strange nobleman nodded and the king continued. "Should you win all three of these events, I will grant one wish to you." The prince bowed, and the king dismissed him to be guided to his quarters.

The feast was held the next day, and the food was indeed great to behold. But the prince did not eat with his hands but withdrew from his sash a pair of wooden sticks that were pointed on one end and dull on the other. Positioning them like claws in his hand, he ate his meal in that fashion, much to the surprise of the court.

All doubt that had been in the king's mind until then was gone in that instant. The prince not only looked different, he acted different!

The first event was an archery competition among the younger nobles. When Thione's turn came, he walked calmly to the line and gazed at the target two hundred yards away. Yet to the surprise of the courtiers he shook his head, and cutting himself a small branch, he wound it into a wreath barely the size of his palm. Espying a page, he commanded the boy to nail the wreath to the center of the target. The boy obeyed, and Thione carefully chose an arrow and aimed but for a moment before shooting. The king could not believe his eyes, for there was the arrow right in the center of the wreath.

Turning to his wife, the queen, he asked, "Do you yet doubt? He is the best that I have ever seen!" Yet the queen was not convinced, and so it came time for the second event. It was a chess match, Thione against the king.

It was a long game that lasted till midday. Finally, using strategies that the king had never seen before, the prince won the game.

It was then decided that the third event would be held the next day. So the king went to bed more mystified than ever.

The next day all woke early for the final test. Sir Mark, the strongest man, was selected to challenge the foreign nobleman in a wrestling match.

The boundaries were marked and Thione and Sir Mark faced each other, listening for the command from the king to begin. The sharp call cracked through the air. Mark lunged for the strangely clad figure. Yet every time he lunged toward the stranger, the prince seemed to disappear and would turn up in the least expected places, doling out small kicks and slaps while never receiving a blow himself. Sir Mark grew angrier and soon his blows were going wide.

That was when the stings became blows and Sir Mark admitted defeat.

Amazed, the king congratulated Thione upon his three victories, saying, "Now you have proven your skill, wisdom, and strength, therefore one wish I shall grant you. Reveal your desire."

The stranger looked at him and to his amazement drew off his helmet, and though once tied back, Lady Thione's hair cascaded down in golden showers and she curtsied. Then she said, "I am Lord Paul's wife. You have sworn to me one wish. That wish is that you release my husband, for in his boastings he never thought to slander your queen."

Then the king laughed, and its merry sound echoed throughout the hall, and he commanded his guards to release Lord Paul, for his folly had been amended.

Then was a great feast held, and Lady Thione met her bewildered husband, and he was glad, and his joy was full and without loneliness. And so they lived happily ever after.

Storm Dancer

by Veronica Engler, age 13

I GAZED OUT from the ferry, my eyes growing big as we neared the island. It shone like an emerald in the morning sunlight, green trees waving to me in greeting. I could not help but smile. What a wonderful way to spend our vacation—my first time seeing the ocean and we were going to be right in the middle of it!

The ferry docked and my family and I disembarked, all four of us dressed in pastels and dragging bulging suitcases. From the moment I stepped onto the pier I was captivated by the regal splendor of the island. The beaches were carpeted with sand white as sugar and the ocean swelled in a blue rhythm. Clouds began to gather above the water, blocking out the sun every so often. It all seemed so wonderful to me.

My family checked into the hotel and dropped off our luggage. The hotel was luxurious, with soft mattresses and royal crimson and gold decorating our rooms. My brother was completely enthralled by the satellite TV, but my favorite part of the room was the floor-to-ceiling window along the west wall. It overlooked

Veronica was living in Gilbert, Arizona, when her story appeared in the July/August 2005 issue of Stone Soup.

THE STONE SOUP BOOK

the ocean and it thrilled me to think that I could watch the tides come in and go out. I stood by the window, watching the swells rise and sink, finally gaining enough momentum to rise high enough to touch the cloud-heavy sky and then cave in on themselves in a chaos of foam and saltwater. I was hypnotized by it, and as the cold blue caressed the white sand, it seemed to me that the ocean was breathing. In fact, I fancied I saw a figure in the waves as they collapsed into the surf, a figure dancing and moving to the ocean's pulse...

"Shelia?"

I jumped at my mom's call and turned to look at her. The entire family was clustered around the door.

"Well, are you coming with us for the tour or what?"

"Yeah—I'm coming!" I said, jumping up to join them.

My mother shook her head as we left the room, muttering, "I swear—sometimes you just get lost in your own head."

"THIS—AS YOU can all see, I'm sure—is the ocean."

The guide swept his hand across the horizon. We all nodded and smiled, adjusting our hats and sunglasses. My family was just a small part of a group of tourists standing on the pier, who came to see the famous Dancer Island. The air was filled with clicks and flashes of light as people took pictures of the setting sun. Not that it was easy to see the sun, with all the clouds.

"Now," said the tour guide, a man named Eddie in his early twenties, "does anyone know why this island is called Dancer Island?"

Everyone shook their heads. My brother, recognizing the beginning of a story, groaned, but I leaned against the railing to get more comfortable. I loved stories and this sounded like an especially good one.

"Hundreds of years ago there lived a woman here who danced to the ocean. It's said that she could change the ocean's mood—could tame it into a gentle babe or stir it up into a frenzy. She was called the Storm Dancer."

The Storm Dancer, I thought, visions of a beautiful woman dancing to the ocean, auburn hair caught up by the wind and eyes blue as the ocean playing through my mind. What a mysterious and exciting name!

"The villagers living here at that time, though, were pretty superstitious. They called her a witch and sentenced her to death. Burned her at the stake."

The crowd around me gasped. What a terrible thing to do to a person! And all because of a little superstition!

Eddie straightened his hat and continued.

"That's not all. After her death, this island had the worst hurricane it's ever seen. Wiped out the entire population. Weren't any people living here until about fifty years later, when someone came off the mainland to start a tourist spot here. And even after that, people say they've seen her dancing on the beach when there's a storm—dancing to the beat of the ocean."

I was spellbound. I wondered if perhaps the dancer saw the ocean the way I did. I wondered if she felt its breathing and the swells seeming to rise and fall to the beat of her own heart just as I did...

"Well, folks, you should be getting back to your hotels now—the weather changes fast around here. Looks like rain," said Eddie and as he spoke a drop of rain fell. A light drizzle started, growing heavier with every second.

"Come on!" I heard my father yell. "Let's get back to the hotel—fast!"

I nodded and began to walk toward the town, but it was raining much harder now. I couldn't see anything in the rain—it was coming down in sheets. I felt for the railing, thinking it would lead me back to the town. The wood was slick and I had to inch my way along. Damp and cold, dripping wet, I found the end of the boardwalk. I took a step forward and slipped, tumbling down in the storm and rain.

I landed in something gritty and soft. I opened my eyes and found somehow I had ended up on the beach. I sat up and found myself staring at the ocean—a raging, screaming ocean that lashed out at me. Its rhythm was no longer slow and steady but angry and unpredictable. Waves rose fierce and black, crashing down in a brawl with the wet sand. The spray hit me full in the face, and I gasped at the overwhelming saltwater.

I cried out and pulled away from the water, trying to crawl away from it. But it followed me, shoving me underneath with damp fury and wrapping me in a chilling embrace. It dragged me further into the clashing elements. I screamed, sobbing with fear, unable to see anything or crawl to safety.

And then in the middle of all the confusion, feet embedded in white sand, skirt whipping about her ankles and auburn hair tossed by the wind, was a woman. She fixed her cool gray-blue eyes on me. I gasped.

She looked away from me and turned to the ocean. She began to sway to a beat and then to dance. She danced like nothing I'd ever seen before, body moving, hips swaying, head held high, mouth whispering verses I could not hear. Her dance was fast, frenzied, to the breathing of the ocean. She danced closer and closer to me, the screaming waves not frightening her or interfering with her dance at all.

Finally, she stopped before me and held out her hand, staring at me with those unnerving eyes. Wordlessly, I took her hand and she pulled me to my feet. Then she began to dance again, swaying to the waves and fury of the water. I closed my eyes, feeling the frantic tempo in my blood rushing through me and I put my hands up and danced.

I was a part of the ocean, a part of its heartbeat, moving to its rhythm. The saltwater did not bother me anymore—the shifting sand beneath my feet no longer a hindrance.

The Storm Dancer and I danced together for what seemed centuries until the ocean began to slow, falling back into its usual regularity. And as it slowed, so did we, until we swayed and stepped one last time and stopped. I looked out at the ocean, the swells friendly and gentle again, the clouds beginning to disappear.

I turned to the Storm Dancer. She didn't smile, but she nodded in approval.

"Shelia! *Shelia!*"

The call of my name made me look up. My mother was standing on the boardwalk, looking down at me. Her eyes were wide with worry and she raced down the steps to get to me.

I turned to the Storm Dancer. She smiled, holding a finger to her lips. Her eyes sparkled like the sun reflecting off her beloved ocean as she turned and walked into the waves, her footsteps not disturbing the water. A wall of saltwater rose before her and closed around her. When it settled, she was gone.

"*Shelia!* Oh, Shelia!"

My mother rushed to me, holding my soaked body close to her.

"Oh, Shelia, poor baby—what are you doing here? We've been looking for you all night!"

"I got lost," I said, watching the ocean swell and collapse, swell and collapse.

"Let's get you back to the hotel," my mother said, pulling me toward the steps. "Everyone will be so glad you've been found."

As we climbed the steps, I chanced a look back at the ocean. In the falling waves, the cold blue shimmering in the emerging sunlight, I fancied I saw a figure in the water, eyes closed, dancing and moving to the rhythm of the ocean.

The Time Magicians

by Casey Tolan, age 13

IT WAS THE MORNING after Gareth had arrived at his Uncle Turif's cabin on the island of Belmopan. The cabin was in a clearing of the isolated Zel Forest, and Turif lived there alone.

Gareth was there against his wishes. Dinner the night before had been a silent, simple meal of meat and greens, and his uncle had turned out to be cold and grouchy.

But that wasn't the worst of it: Gareth had seen Turif do Time Magic.

As he lay in the chair that had been his bed, Gareth thought back to the day before, when Turif had used his Magic to speed up a tree in Time, causing it to age and then die in a minute. Gareth shuddered. Time Magic was believed to be evil.

Gareth's father, Seramon, always said that Turif was the black sheep of the family. With cold eyes, Seramon would tell of the day he had found Turif practicing Time Magic, playing with Time itself.

"Bad stuff, Time Magic is," said Seramon. "Normal magic's

Casey was living in Shorewood, Wisconsin, when his story appeared in the January/February 2007 issue of Stone Soup.

fine and all; it's OK. Time Magic, though, well you want to keep clear of that. Messing with Time, you never can tell what's going to happen." Luckily for Seramon, Turif was one of the few Time Magicians left in the known world, if not the only one.

Gareth stretched, and listened for any telltale sound that Turif was awake. He heard nothing, and tiptoed across the hall into the kitchen to find something to eat; he decided upon a juicy red apple. He bit into it as he tiptoed back across the kitchen—colliding with the scowling Turif.

"Stealing now, are we?" said Turif dryly, stepping past Gareth and into the kitchen. He grabbed a loaf of bread for himself.

"I... I..." Gareth stood there, looking at the apple. "I wasn't trying to steal, U-Uncle. I was just... hungry."

Turif snorted, munching on the bread. "Well, that apple's your breakfast, boy," said Turif. He walked outside into the clearing, calling, "Follow me."

Turif sat on the trunk of a fallen tree, and motioned for Gareth to do the same. "Boy," he said, taking a deep breath, "you have potential."

"What?"

Turif sighed. "Has your father told you nothing?" he muttered.

The boy blinked.

"You're a Time Magician. Well, not a Time Magician in full," frowned Turif, considering.

"Wait," said Gareth. "I'm..." he coughed, "I'm a Time Magician?"

"Are you listening, boy?" hissed Turif. "You have the potential to become one! And I'm going to make sure that that potential is fulfilled."

"I... I don't understand."

Turif stood up and began to pace in irritation. "With my help, you can become a Time Magician," he said slowly and with a calm that threatened to break at any second. "Then you and I will be the only two Time Magicians in the world."

"Well, do I have to be one?" asked Gareth, not fully comprehending the situation.

Turif roared with irritation. He swung his hand in the air, causing the fleeting sound of a stream. Then, everything stopped.

Except for Turif and Gareth, the world was frozen. Butterflies were suspended in the air. The wind ceased to blow, and the birds were silent and held unnaturally still.

"That," said Turif quietly, "is what you will do when I finish with you."

Gareth understood.

Still, he was divided. Part of him wanted to accept Turif's offer, wanted the power of Time Magic. The other heard the echo of his father's voice: "Bad stuff, Time Magic is..."

As the clearing around him came back into motion, Gareth worried that Seramon was right. Turif was interfering with Time itself, and although it was amazing, it was also terrible.

"Sorry," replied Gareth, "but I can't be a Time Magician."

Turif stared at him.

"I'm not asking you if you want to," he said, anger edging his voice again. "You will be a Time Magician: when I die, the art of Time Magic will die with me if you aren't. And I'm not about to let that happen."

Without waiting for a response from Gareth, he stood.

"Your lessons will begin now."

Gareth began to argue, but Turif's glare made him decide to cooperate, for now.

"First, you must learn about The River of Time," Turif said. "It is everywhere, always there, always flowing. Normally, The River flows at a certain speed, and everything is drawn along with it. All Time Magic really does is manipulate it.

"What a Time Magician needs to do is change The River's speed. If you can make it go faster, Time goes faster. And vice versa. You can also make it stop flowing. The only thing you cannot do to The River is reverse it. You cannot go back to the past.

"People around the Magician, even those who are not

Magicians themselves, hear The River flow when Time Magic is used."

"That's what I heard yesterday when you sped up the tree!" exclaimed Gareth, excited despite himself. Turif nodded, and continued.

"You never change all of The River. That would take enough power to kill a Magician. What you have to do is manipulate parts of it. For instance, when I stopped Time just now, Time outside of the clearing didn't stop moving. And we weren't frozen in place.

"Time Magic can also have disastrous results. For instance, if I had let Time escape my control it could have frozen the entire forest. Time Magic can be very dangerous.

"And now it's time for you to try feeling The River."

Gareth admitted that Time Magic sounded amazing, but he remembered what Seramon had said. He would pretend to go along, and maybe Turif would forget the whole thing.

"Sit still," said Turif. "Close your eyes. Don't move. Don't talk. Don't even think. Try to feel The River flowing around you."

Gareth did as he was told, although he was starting to feel a little silly. He tried not to think, but his mind kept wandering. He had to use all of his concentration to think of nothing.

Suddenly, he felt something around him. It felt like water, currents and eddies. He yelped, his concentration shattered.

"I... I felt it," he stammered, his eyes wide. "It felt like water!"

"It was The River," said Turif. "Try again."

After concentrating for a while, Gareth felt it once more. This time, he didn't let The River surprise him. But the longer he concentrated, the harder it got. Finally, he let go of his concentration and opened his eyes, panting. It felt like he had been concentrating for ages.

"That was less than a half minute!" frowned Turif. "You have to be able to do better than that. Try again."

For the next hour or so, Gareth practiced holding onto his concentration. At the end, he was tired, even though he hadn't been fully trying and his concentration never lasted longer than a minute.

Turif was disappointed.

"Well," he said, "it'll have to be good enough. Now, you'll try to control The River." He walked around the clearing, and eventually came back with a fallen tree branch, which he placed next to Gareth. "First, feel The River in your mind."

Gareth concentrated, and soon felt it.

"Now, sense the branch, sense how The River is pulling it along. Sense how the branch is aging in Time."

Gareth thought hard, and surprisingly, he could subconsciously feel The River flowing around the branch.

"Feel each eddy and each current," continued Turif. "Then take hold of one of those currents."

Gareth felt the eddies and the currents, but when he tried to take hold of one, his concentration broke.

"Try harder!" yelled Turif, irritated. "Catch the currents with your mind, boy! That's the magic of it, the reaching out with your mind. You have potential; you can do it. Pretend that your mind is another hand. Reach out with it, but only when your concentration is complete."

Gareth tried again, but failed. In the end, he was totally exhausted.

"Hmmmmm..." muttered Turif, thinking. Then an idea came to him. "Maybe the branch is too big. Go take a rest and have a snack, then come back here and we'll try again."

Obliging, Gareth went to the cabin. In a few moments, he was asleep in a chair.

AFTER GARETH WOKE up and had another apple, he decided to try again. Even though he didn't intend to become a Time Magician, he was curious.

"Let's try something small," said Turif, picking a blade of grass and setting it on the tree trunk next to Gareth, who eyed it incredulously. A blade of grass?

"When we finish training today, you will be able to make this blade of grass wither far faster than it would normally. Now, do what you have been doing, but concentrate harder."

Gareth concentrated, but immediately felt nauseous.

"Ohhhhhhhhh… " He moaned in pain and discomfort.

"Stop groaning, boy," shouted Turif. "You're just feeling the aftereffects of using Time Magic! Once you're used to it, you won't feel anything. Now concentrate!"

Mad at Turif for yelling at him, Gareth wanted to prove that he could do it. He tried again and again, but failed each time; the nausea got worse as he kept trying. Turif egged him on, and didn't let him stop until well past noon. Gareth was exhausted, angry, and sick.

"Pitiful," spat Turif disgustedly, shaking his head. "When I was your age, I could stop Time for minutes on end without getting sick at all. You're weak, just like your father."

Then Gareth cracked.

"How dare you!" he shouted at Turif, jumping up in rage. "My father isn't weak, and neither am I! Who cares about Time Magic, who cares if you're the last Time Magician in the world?"

For a second, a shocked look came over Turif's face. Then anger replaced it.

"What are you going to do, then, boy?" he hissed. "Without me, you'd be in the middle of a brewing war! You'll do as I say. Sit down and be quiet, now, or you'll regret it!"

Gareth was too angry to do anything. He seethed and stood eye to eye with Turif. It was as if Turif had stopped Time again.

Gareth turned away. Anger boiling within, he stomped from the clearing, not knowing where he was going; somewhere, anywhere was better than being with Turif.

He crashed through the foliage. He decided he wouldn't stop until he got to the edge of Belmopan, and then he would run and run and run all the way across the Vanere Sea and back to his parents in Daria, his home.

But a war was brewing on the mainland, between his home

country of Aargaria and their age-old enemies, the Nadere Empire.

Because of the danger, Seramon and Gareth's mother, Tara, had sent Gareth away to the neutral island of Belmopan, where Turif lived. Although Seramon hated Turif, he was the family's only relative, and he would (hopefully) keep Gareth safe.

But now, he ran and ran and...

Smack! Gareth ran straight into what seemed to be a strange-shaped tree. He backed away, rubbing his bruised forehead, and prepared to run on. But then the tree started to move.

It arranged itself, and turned to face Gareth. It was a huge, catlike thing with dark brown fur, which gave it the impression of a tree trunk. Its eyes were golden and full of anger at being awoken. It yelped, and jumped at Gareth.

Fear paralyzed him. As the cat bore down on him, all he could do was watch in terror. And then...

The cat-thing stopped in midleap, less than a foot away from Gareth's face. It was frozen in Time, along with a small area of forest. Gareth was also frozen, and this time not with fear.

Turif stepped into the frozen space slowly, keeping a bubble of moving Time around him.

"What have you gotten yourself into now, boy?" he asked with a hint of laughter. He came level with Gareth, and looked at him, considering.

"Why did you run off like that?" Gareth could not answer, of course. "Cat's got your tongue?" laughed Turif.

He pushed the cat-thing down, until it was lying on the ground. Then he released his hold on The River around Gareth, letting him move once again. The cat-thing, however, was still frozen.

"Y-You saved me," he breathed, checking himself, making sure he was all right.

"Now do you believe in the power of Time Magic?" asked Turif, smiling slightly.

"Uncle Turif," said Gareth, "I felt the magic when you froze

Time. I should have trusted you when you said I have potential."

"I suppose I've been too hard on you," replied Turif. "It's just that... well, after spending many years by myself, I sort of forgot how to be kind. And I couldn't let you not become a Time Magician.

"Now," he continued, "let's go back to the cabin and call it a day. Tomorrow we'll start practicing again."

"I promise I'll do my best!" said Gareth.

They left the spot, Turif letting the Time Magic go. The cat-thing lay on the ground, confused and disoriented. It curled up, and went to sleep once more.

FOR THE NEXT few days, Turif and Gareth practiced. The former was trying to be kinder, and the latter was giving it his all. No longer was dinner silent, and the two were starting to become friends. Gareth even read a few of the books on Time Magic in Turif's library, and was getting better and better at the art.

Three days after the cat-thing incident, the message bird arrived. It alighted on Turif's arm. "Turif Arnolged Pastest. One message for Turif Arnolged Pastest. Would that be you?" Its voice was loud and surprisingly nasal.

Message birds did not literally carry messages like homing pigeons, with the note tied around their legs. Instead, the sender of the message related it to the bird, and the bird remembered the message. Then using some unknown magic, it found the message's recipient and recited it.

"Yes..." replied Turif to the bird, sounding concerned.

"This message is from Queen Elisa Barona Simonia." Gareth's eyes grew wide. The Queen of Belmopan? Turif obviously had some secrets.

"Message begins: Turif! Nadere has officially declared war. I must send our troops to Aargaria to aid them. Come to the castle at once. I will deploy the troops in one hour whether you are here or not. Aargaria must be helped! Message ends."

For a second, there was silence. Turif was numb with shock,

and Gareth was confused, trying to figure out the strange message.

The message bird broke their silence. "Will there be a reply message?"

Turif jumped into action, tossing the bird into the air. "Tell her I will be there and that she must not enter the war! Now go! Fly fast!" He ran into the cabin. The message bird fluttered around, then took off, muttering something about humans that did not sound like a compliment.

"What was that about?" Gareth asked Turif, following him into the kitchen. Turif was packing a bag of food for himself.

He said hurriedly, "Gareth, you must stay here. Do not leave the clearing until I return. I'll probably be gone overnight, but you'll be fine. I'll see you soon." Before Gareth could ask more, Turif ran through the house and out of the clearing, already formulating a spell to make Time around him flow faster.

Gareth stood there, not knowing what to do. He thought of what the message bird had said. "Nadere has officially declared war. I must send troops to Aargaria." Something clicked in his mind.

Nadere had declared war on Aargaria.

And Daria, his home, would soon be in the middle of a war zone.

Miles and miles away from the conflict, Gareth felt helpless, totally helpless. How could he help stop Nadere from attacking his homeland? He was only a child; he had no power.

Or did he?

Gareth knew what he needed to do.

He ran through the house and grabbed his bag, some food, a canteen of water, and—after a slight hesitation—one of Turif's Time Magic books.

Gareth looked around the cabin once more. He took a deep breath, then stepped into the clearing.

Aargaria was waiting.

Gareth was coming.

Makoto, the Turtle Boy

by Annakai Hayakawa Geshlider, age 11

T HERE WAS ONCE a boy who lived in a village in a valley of Japan. His village had wooden houses with sliding doors and rushing water and creeks. One hot summer day, it rained heavily from dawn to dusk. The creeks got deeper and wilder, and the boy, Makoto, thought it was the perfect time to venture down to the creek and hop from rock to rock. Makoto loved to watch the water, to feel it gushing over his hands. He put on a finely woven straw hat and his blue shoes.

Makoto's mother was fixing lunch, and she told him to be back in half an hour so he could eat with his father when he came home from his job at the post office. Makoto told his mother that he would be back by then.

Stretching his socks up to his knees so he would not get mosquito bites, Makoto started down the road. Not many others were on the road at the time, but Makoto did not mind. He liked to be by himself, to breathe in the fresh, thick air, to wade in the creek, to trek amongst the large green trees of the valley. School

Annakai was living in San Francisco, California, when her story appeared in the September/October 2006 issue of Stone Soup.

THE STONE SOUP BOOK

had just ended, and Makoto went out every day to see something new, or to visit old special places.

Makoto headed down the road, and stopped at the post office to say hello to his dad. Makoto reached into his pocket and took out a few pumpkin seeds. He handed them to his dad over the counter where he worked, selling people stamps or arranging for their letters and packages to be mailed. Makoto pressed the seeds into his father's hand and his father smiled and thanked him.

"Where are you off to today?" he asked Makoto.

"The creek," Makoto told him. Then, in a hurry to get there, Makoto waved to his father and ran down the rest of the road.

Makoto walked past the giant bamboo stalks and he stepped carefully down to the creek. He hopped from rock to rock, and then stopped to listen to the loud, rushing water. He looked to his right, where two waterfalls stood. They had been there for hundreds of years. He hopped onto three more rocks, slipping on the last one, which was wet and slippery. He fell on it and scraped his knee, and as he scrambled up on the opposite bank, his shoe was pulled from his foot and swept down the river. Makoto ran down the riverbank as fast as he could. He caught up with his shoe, but then it floated away from him and under the bridge. There was no bank for him to run on and no rocks to hop on. He waded into the creek, then swam through the creek and under the bridge. His shoe had caught in between two rocks. He swam closer to it, but was soon swept off to the side. Makoto was tired from swimming and his limbs were sore. He pulled himself up onto the bank, and lay down on his side. He was wearing only one shoe. He turned to lie down on his back on the muddy bank. He sat for a long while, just thinking and sitting still. Then he remembered that he had been asked to be home to eat lunch with his father.

His shoe was no longer in sight and Makoto was so tired that he couldn't bring himself to swim through the rushing water and the sharp rocks. He decided that he would sit on the bank until a villager noticed him. But if he didn't arrive home soon, his parents would be worried.

Makoto was just falling asleep when he heard an ancient voice whisper into his ear. "I will take you back, and look! I found your shoe." Makoto opened one eye and then two. A turtle was standing in the mud next to him. On the turtle's back was his shoe! Makoto thanked him gratefully and put his shoe back onto his foot.

The turtle waded into the water. "Climb onto my back," he said. Makoto sat down on the turtle's back and he leaned forward and held on tight to the turtle's beautiful shell. Then the turtle swam swiftly into the water.

Makoto held his breath, but the turtle assured him that he didn't need to. Makoto breathed in, and water came out his nose. "I wasn't ever able to breathe water before!" he told the turtle.

The turtle smiled wisely and said to Makoto, "Did you ever try?"

Makoto had not.

The turtle said to him, "Makoto, you have always been one of us. You are really a human body and mind, but your spirit and soul are turtle. Once every seven years we give one newborn child the ability. The child can breathe and swim like us. When you fell into the creek when you were young, all the turtles of the creek circled around you to cast the spell. Your mother came and took you out of the water just after you had become part turtle."

Makoto was amazed with the turtle's tale, and he believed it. He even found himself about to check if there was a shell on his back, but he remembered that his appearance was human. He began to get used to breathing water, and soon they had swum under the bridge. The turtle paddled in between rocks, and then up the bank. Makoto turned to say goodbye and thank you to the turtle.

But the turtle had swum back into the creek.

Makoto crossed the creek on the rocks once again, and he held on with his hands so that he didn't slip. He hurried up to the road and ran toward his house. His slid open the door and took off his shoes. He slipped into his house slippers and crossed the room to the table where his parents were sitting on the tatami mats.

Maikua

by Josh Miller, age 10

ONCE THERE WAS a strong woman who was great at hunting, fishing, and all the other manly things. But she didn't have the patience to learn the delicate art of sewing baskets, dyeing clothes, or any of the things the women did.

Her name was Maikua.

Maikua had flowing black hair, and brown eyes and skin.

None of the men liked Maikua. When she went hunting with them, they would say, "We don't need your help. Why don't you go home."

Maikua never listened to these men. She would go out and catch as many birds as she could carry. When they got home, the other men and women would fill their stomachs with her catch and leave the scraps for her.

The other women didn't think much of her either. Whenever she stayed home when the men were hunting (which wasn't very often), the women would say, "Why aren't you out hunting? Maybe if you tried harder you could catch a piece of fur."

Josh was living in Portland, Oregon, when his story appeared in the May/June 2005 issue of Stone Soup.

THE STONE SOUP BOOK

Maikua would just ignore them, and go on shooting her bows and arrows at a practice target.

One day Maikua went out fishing. She caught eight fish, and put them in her basket. When she returned to the village, though, the usual commotion was no more. In fact, she couldn't see anybody for miles. "Is anybody here?" she called out.

The response was, "Is anybody here?" It was just an echo.

Maikua realized that everybody had left. She went back to her hut and ate the fresh fish. Then she thought. "Maybe I should go to the mystic mountain," she said to herself.

She set out at dawn. The mountain reached out over the treetops.

Maikua started walking. She swam across a river. She swung on vines and she leapt over roots. Finally the mountain lay before her: glowing green trees, gray rocks, and pure white snow.

Maikua got out her spear. She sighted a mountain lion in the distance. She crept up the mountainside, and then hid behind a boulder so the lion couldn't see her. She took a piece of meat out of her basket, and put it out in front of the boulder. The lion ran over and clamped its teeth around the meat. As soon as he did so Maikua had the spear through his head.

Maikua had a good lunch and then was on her way.

When Maikua got to the top of the mountain, she found a bear. The bear gave her a cup made out of leaves. The bear said, "Drink the water that lies in the cup."

As she drank, a stairway started forming. When the last drop of water was finished, the stairway reached all the way to the tip of the clouds. The bear motioned for her to climb the stairs.

When Maikua got to the top of the stairs, she couldn't speak. Not just because there was a village before her; but because in this village, she saw women coming home with fish and deer, and men sitting in their huts weaving baskets and taking care of the young ones.

A woman walked over to Maikua.

"Who are you?" Maikua asked.

"I am Korto, the head of our village," the woman answered. "Let me show you around."

Korto showed Maikua her hut and the meat storage room and more. After the tour Maikua asked, "Why are things so different here?"

"This is the way it has always been," Korto said, "for as long as I can remember. Now you should get some sleep. You look very tired."

Maikua walked slowly back to her hut. She was thinking about this strange yet wonderful village as she climbed through the door of the hut and curled up on her bed.

After a week Maikua was already a hero. The men adored her, and the women looked up to her. She filled the meat storage room with fish and game she had caught, and was happier than she had ever been. But a few weeks later, she announced that it was time to leave.

The night before Maikua was to leave there was a big celebration. The finest meats were prepared, and toasts were made. There was singing and dancing. The noise was very powerful. At the end of the evening, Korto called everyone to attention. Everyone stood in a circle, facing Korto. She sat straight in her chair, and then said, "I think we owe Maikua a wish." Everyone cheered.

Maikua was stunned.

"What is your wish?" Korto asked.

Maikua thought for a moment, then exclaimed, "I know what I want. I want to never run out of arrows."

"Everlasting arrows, eh? I'll see what I can do," Korto smiled. Then she pointed her finger at Maikua and a bag appeared on Maikua's shoulder—a bag filled with arrows.

Maikua thanked everybody and went back to her hut. She went to sleep. But around midnight she snuck out of bed with the bag on her shoulders, and headed back down the stairway out of the clouds.

When she came out of the clouds back into her own world,

the first thing she saw was smoke coming out of the treetops. Maikua ran as fast as she could down the mountain and into a forest. She came into a clearing and saw people. They were her people, her town in rags, sitting around a fire.

When the people saw her they were so happy they crowded around her, hugging her.

"You're back!" they shouted.

"What's happening?" Maikua asked.

A man came up to her and said, "We need you. Your skills keep us alive."

Maikua didn't know what to say. She was so happy that they had accepted her. All the women and the men apologized and welcomed Maikua back.

From then on, hunting was valued in men and in women.

Secrets in the Forest

by Eleyna Rosenthal, age 13

CASPING PEERED OUT of the curtains hiding her in the carriage speeding down a gravel road. A guard on the seat beside her grunted and reached over to pull her back inside. With a sigh of grief and understanding, Casping sat back against the silk-covered seat. She hung her head and let the burning sensation behind her eyes ascend. She let her soft blond hair cover her pale, angelic face as she wept.

The carriage took a sharp turn, stopping her in the middle of a sob. She quickly reminded herself this was all for the best. She needed to stay hidden, and stay safe. Death was not an option; she needed to survive long enough to rule her parents' kingdom. If she did not hide, then surely her family's enemy, the powerful Rasha, would find and kill her. Casping knew she must accept her fate. Besides, her family must really love her to go to these measures of safety. Casping shivered as the cold winter wind blew open the curtains. She caught a glimpse of frost-covered trees and bushes and wondered what it would be like living in the

Eleyna was living in Media, Pennsylvania, when her story appeared in the November/December 2006 issue of Stone Soup.

middle of a deserted forest. At least she would have a cabin to live in and the two guards riding beside her to protect her.

Sighing, now out of boredom and impatience, Casping turned to ask the guard on her right how much longer it would be. Suddenly an arrow came flying through the curtains as they burst into flames. The arrow was on fire! It struck the guard in the chest and he immediately fell. Casping let out a terrified scream, jumping up in panic. She turned to find her left guard was already dead as well. She turned her wide silver eyes to the man who was leading the horses. He was slumped over in the seat, bleeding from a very recent wound.

Casping's heart seemed to stop, but her mind didn't. She jumped into the front seat and pushed the body out of the way with a muttered "Sorry." She urged the horses into a full gallop. Racing down a slope, she could hear more arrows being shot towards her, and the orange flames just missing her. As the carriage suddenly erupted into flames, Casping knew she was done for. She saw her only chance of escape to her left. It was a forest, dark and mysterious. Everything seemed to slow down as she jumped out of the carriage. She rapidly undid the leather straps connecting the horses to the carriage and jumped atop the one who was the fastest, Kundra. The other horse ran in the opposite direction, towards the enemy. Casping cringed as she heard it let out a last whinny, but she didn't stop. She coaxed Kundra into a blinding run towards any ounce of safety the forest held and prayed they'd make it.

The moon was already up by the time Casping was sure she and Kundra were alone. The over-exercised horse's sides were heaving as he wheezed. Casping staggered off the sweaty black horse.

Tying up Kundra by his bridle, she murmured soft words: "There, there, good boy. It'll be all right." Her once melodic voice was now oozing with mental pain and emptiness. Kundra whinnied hoarsely in reply. A strong wind began to blow, sending shivers to caress Casping. Clouds overhead were as dark as thick smoke and full of threatening snow. Only moments later, the promised snow began to glide down to earth. In an attempt to shield herself from winter's unforgiving embrace, Casping pulled her soft robe over her head. Kundra was sleeping by the time Casping had created a reasonably warm fire. She knew she could not cry, for the water might freeze her face even more. Instead, she lay down beside the fire and gratefully gave herself up to her dreams.

It must have been in the wee hours of the morning when Casping woke up. Something was wrong. She never woke up this early without a reason. Then the sound that had awakened her repeated. It was howling. The howl sounded like it was coming from one lonely wolf. "Calm down, Kundra. I won't let it hurt you," Casping whispered, trying to soothe the panicking horse. He bucked, then froze with wide, rolling eyes. "What is..." Casping began to ask, but a growl interrupted her from a few yards at least behind her. Kundra yanked on his bridle, cutting his mouth on the bit. Casping untied the reins, about to ride him out of the forest. But, with other intentions, Kundra sped off into the woods.

Casping heard the trample of hooves on the undergrowth and howling that was moving towards the trampling. Suddenly, a sickening whinny sounded across the forest to Casping, making her cringe. She wanted to run after Kundra, bring him back to safety, but feared what she would see. Fearful of the wolf's return, she built up another fire and fell into a freezing sleep.

Movement woke Casping. She opened her eyes in a confused daze. She couldn't feel her face! What was going on? Her fingers were stiff and felt frozen. Casping finally realized someone was carrying her. She looked into an unfamiliar face. He was handsome and young, only a few years older-looking than her. He looked down at her, concern in his sharp eyes. His eyes were odd. They were golden brown colors, but that wasn't the odd part. They didn't look very... human. After a few minutes, or so it seemed, Casping realized she was in a hut, and a very warm and cozy hut at that. She was placed on a soft blanket, one made of brown fur. The stranger had his back turned to her. She watched him weakly, feeling some warmth creeping around in her body. He turned around, watching her intently, almost studying her. She looked away and felt her eyes grow heavy. Before she knew what was going on, the stranger was putting some foul-tasting syrup into her mouth and making her swallow it. Everything was getting fuzzy because her vision was blurring. She could feel him watching her, though. She wanted to sit upright and yell at him to turn his eyes away, but all she could do was get a moan out of her mouth and then sleep overcame her.

Casping awoke to find herself alone. Her head throbbed and her throat felt parched. She opened her eyes slowly, and then blinked a few times. Lying there for a moment, just looking up at the wooden ceiling, Casping tried sitting up. To her relief she found she could with almost no pain. She sat upright, taking in her surroundings. Once she felt sure she was alone and safe for now, she stood up on wobbly legs. She used the only table in the large hut to help keep her balance.

A loud creaking sound erupted behind her. She turned around almost too fast to find that unfamiliar stranger facing her. He looked surprised, as if he didn't assume she would wake up. Over his shoulder was a leather bag stuffed with furry animals Casping could not make out.

Casping reached for her pocket, only now remembering she had a sheathed knife at her side. Only then did she realize it was missing. She looked around frantically in case she had dropped it. Seeing it was nowhere within sight, Casping turned on the stranger while looking for any other ways to escape besides the door, which he blocked. There was none.

"Whoa, calm down. Why would I save you just to hurt you?" the stranger asked, obviously taking in Casping's protective stance.

Casping didn't reply immediately. After studying her "savior," she straightened up to look more like the princess she was. "I am

Princess Casping," she replied with a confident voice and shaking hands. "I demand to know who you are and where I am… and why I am here." She crossed her arms to show she meant business.

"First of all, I answer to no one's demands; I am not a servant for the royal household. I will tell you my name, and not because you asked, but because I was planning to tell you anyway. I am Troyce. To answer your next question, I would expect it is obvious you are in the forest on the edge of your kingdom." Troyce paused here to close the door as a cold wind came towards the hut. He turned around again to answer the last question. "As to why you were in the forest in the first place, I haven't a clue. But, I brought you here because you were going to freeze. Plus, you no longer… had means of transportation," he concluded with a sly grin that made Casping want to ask a hundred more questions.

It took a few minutes for Casping to register all of this information. "So, you're saying that you saved me from certain death?" she asked, raising her eyebrows like it was hard to believe.

Troyce only nodded to confirm it. "So, what brings a princess to the forest?" Troyce asked, walking towards Casping and dumping his bag onto the table. "I mean, wouldn't you prefer to sleep in your bedchamber or whatever it is you have…?" he asked, busying himself with unloading the bag.

"For your information, Troyce, I was chased into the forest. By Rasha's men, assuming you know who he is," Casping said, wondering why she felt the need to put scorn in her voice.

Troyce visibly stiffened, and then quickly regained control of his emotions and busied himself again with the bag. "I've heard of him… we all have."

"We?"

"My kind, you know? My family, my friends… my pack," Troyce spoke softly.

"Did you say pack?" Casping questioned with rising frustration resulting from confusion.

"Yeah. It's kind of a long story. You see, well, my pack and I used to live in your kingdom. On Rasha's land to be exact. He didn't like the thought of having 'fantastical' creatures on his land. So he..."

"Whoa, fantastical creatures?" Casping interrupted.

Troyce went on as if she hadn't said a word, "banished us from your kingdom. It's not like he had the right to, but he certainly had enough soldiers to push us off. Even in our other forms we were no match for them," Troyce concluded with a distant look on his face.

"Hold it just one second. What exactly are you if you aren't human?" Casping asked, backing up a little.

"We're werewolves. Not exactly the correct word, but one that'll do us justice I suppose," Troyce stated so calmly, like everyone should know werewolves existed.

Casping stood silently, mouth wide open. Then she burst out laughing. "Thanks, I really needed some humor right now," she said, wiping the back of her hand over her eyes.

Troyce turned to glare at her. "I'm not joking. Perhaps nowadays people need to see to believe." He gave a weary sigh and then his entire body seemed to shimmer and sparkle. Casping watched in mystified horror. Suddenly a blond wolf nearly twice her size was staring back at her with human-like eyes. It growled, causing a shudder to run over Casping. She realized she could run, she could scream, she could try to kill the wolf. But she didn't. She just stood gaping at it, unable to wrench away from Troyce's gaze. Her eyes began to hurt from staring so long and she blinked. When she opened her eyes a second later, Troyce stood beside her as if he had never changed. "See?" he said simply and returned to shuffling the furry animals in the bag. Casping could only watch Troyce in a dreamlike fashion. For some reason, she found it was not hard to believe what Troyce said. Of course she had to believe he was a werewolf, she had just seen it.

"So... you hate Rasha, too?" she asked, wondering if perhaps she had just found a powerful ally for her parents.

"Of course! How could we not? They stole what had been

rightfully ours for thousands of centuries! But we daren't show our faces to him, at least not on our own. We'll be shot down before we can change into our fanged form," Troyce paused and held his breath, as if remembering a painful memory.

"Well... why don't you all partner up with my parents' army? Then Rasha would be no match for us!" Casping exclaimed, eyes lighting up with excited hope. "Wait, how many of your kind are there?" she questioned, seeing that a small number of them would not add much to their army.

"Well, in this forest there are... umm, let's see," he paused for a moment to calculate, "probably a couple hundred, maybe a thousand, and within your kingdom, probably a few more thousand. Also, many packs moved farther north."

Casping jumped up and down like a little girl with a new toy. "Oh, Troyce, don't you see?!" she cried out. "We could come together and rid ourselves of Rasha and his men once and for all! You could gather all the packs up and join the army!"

Troyce stared at her for a moment like she was crazy. Then he smiled faintly and a sly look crossed through his eyes. "Give me a week."

He spoke in a slick voice that made Casping tremble from anticipation of their plan. She knew deep down she had found the answer to her kingdom's prayers. And another soft feeling in her heart told her she had found what she had been seeking all her life, even if she hadn't known it. She was in love with Troyce, but she didn't realize it. Not yet.

Penny's Journey

by Ben Mast, age 12

THE HOLE, sitting there in the middle of the clearing, was by no means small, but the little wide-eyed girl of thirteen years was still amazed that something as big as a dragon could've fit through it.

Penny was a peasant in the town. She had left the city's gates to fetch water for her family when she sighted a strange trail of scales and prints leading off toward the forest. And then she had seen it—a glittering sky-blue dragon with magnificent leathery wings and blazing green eyes. It had been only a second before it had slithered into the burrow in a final flash of radiance.

Now Penny stood beside the hole, her straight profile outlined in the setting sun, confident, but tense—like a tiger waiting to pounce, dirty-blond wisps of her hair escaping from a messy bun in the evening breeze. Her empty water jug lay upturned and forgotten. The people of her city dreaded dragons, their emotions mixed with fear and anger. But even Penny, after seeing a dragon in its most innocent form, could not blame them.

Ben was living in Goshen, Indiana, when his story appeared in the November/December 2005 issue of Stone Soup.

Only thirteen years had passed since the dragons had come.

There had been nine of them, all fiery red, with hot, searing breath and wide, hungry mouths. They had killed Penny's sister, mother, and father. She could not remember any of them, though, because that was the night she was born, two hours before her family was killed. Now, all that remained of her relatives were her uncle, aunt, adopted two-year-old brother, and her grandparents, who all lived in the same mud hut.

Penny raced among the tall, ominous pines and oaks, their snagging branches snatching at her skin and clothing. She only slowed to a steady trot once the trees thinned and she could see the village gates ahead. The village was small and nearly everyone knew everyone. But ever since the fateful day when Penny was born, each person had grown independent and sharp. Penny raced among the small, familiar houses until she saw the tiny mud-brick cottage with a thatched roof that was her own. After murmuring a brief apology for not getting water to her hawkeyed, hands-on-her-hips kind of grandma, she trotted briskly to her small room in search of a good book.

But thoughts of the sky-blue dragon slowly led her to the window, looking out toward the dark forest. Through all of what Penny had experienced in her thirteen short years, she had a will tougher than most young girls. But this—it pulled on her as if by magic and soon she was sprinting toward the wood again. She soon came upon the hole, but this time she didn't stop.

She dove right in, and blackness shrouded over her thoughts.

PENNY WOKE UP feeling like she had eaten too many of Grandma's sweet cakes the night before. Trying in vain to flatten a mess of disheveled hair, she turned her sharp chin to a noise in the door.

There sat the dragon, its glittering eyes focusing on the young girl. Finally, in a deep, throaty voice, he said, "I've been waiting."

Penny sat speechless with wonder. Before she could think of the strangeness of what he had said, he croaked again, "What is your name?"

"Penny."

"Where do you come from?"

"The village." Her voice was barely a whisper.

"Are you scared?"

"Yes."

"I can make you happier." The dragon's eyes seemed to smile. Penny's eyes flared in anger. "Who said I wasn't happy?" she snapped angrily. She stood as if to leave.

"Please," the dragon sighed, rustling his wings. "I am lonely. Stay." And then, "I will show you my world."

"But..." Penny objected, but then a burst of color flashed into her mind. She cried in astonishment, and as more images splashed across her thoughts, she realized that the dragon could not only speak, but he could pass on pictures into another's mind, too. Into Penny's mind sparked dazzling mountains, sparkling rivers, and creatures of all different kinds. And suddenly they stopped. Penny only realized that she was closing her eyes then, and she looked up, blinking, at the dragon, who gave a kind smile back.

"That was... wonderful," Penny stammered quietly.

The dragon stretched his wings, then calmly asked, "Would you like to live there? With me?"

Penny thought of the astounding offer. Her thoughts returned to the pictures—the castles, and treasure, pirates and mermaids and lakes and... everything imaginable. But how? How could there be a place so... perfect? But, she thought, Grandma had always said there was a perfect place—later. But was this what she had meant? Thinking of her grandma made her thoughts whirl to Stefan, the small outcast who her family adopted, his pudgy cheeks and tumbling chuckle. And of tight-lipped Grandma, "pleasingly plump" Aunt Mabel, tall, dangerous-looking Uncle Ted, and old Gramps, who couldn't walk or remember anything. "Not much to speak of," Penny said dismally to herself.

But they were enough.

Her sharp complexion turned toward the dragon and she stated flatly, "I'm sorry. But I refuse."

The dragon let out a strange human-like scream. Then, his textured scales turned into folds of smooth, silky black robes. His green eyes turned dark and dangerous as his snout folded in and a beard sprouted from a jutting chin. And there stood a man—a magician—with an evil glint in his eye.

"Penny, you're the last one of a long line. Your father was the twenty-third in that line and you, the twenty-fourth. If you haven't figured it out by now, I plan to have you eliminated from existence."

She had. Her first instincts told her to turn and run, but she wanted to learn more. "Why are you doing this?" Her voice was confident. The only thing betraying her fear was in her eyes.

"One of your ancient ancestors and I made a deal—and he didn't keep his end of the deal up, as did I. You can figure out the rest. Be assured, it would have been a much slower, more painful death if you had not resisted the temptation to come to 'my world.'"

"Did you send the red dragons to our village the night my family died?" Penny's voice quavered.

"Smart girl."

Penny did not need any further knowledge of the sadistic magician. She turned and bolted for the hole. The wizard raised a finger and it disappeared. Penny turned, helpless, and then dove into a roll, grabbing a handful of sand and throwing it into the magician's face. As he wiped grit from his eyes and spat it out of his mouth, he lost his concentration and the hole reappeared for an instant. It was all Penny needed. She catapulted through, appearing in the middle of the forest. From her position, she could hear the magician clambering through the hole after her, cursing all the while. In a final act of desperation, she took her abandoned water jug and shoved it through the hole, hearing the satisfying clunk of the clay jug meeting the magician's skull.

Without another thought, the girl turned and tore through

the forest all the way to her village. Stopping briefly at the door of her house, she barged in, sighting her grandma, and in a bound swept her off the floor in a big hug.

Their arms entwined and, tears streaming down Penny's grubby face, she cried, "I love you, Grandma. I love you."

River God

by Virginia Mason, age 12

WE SAT THERE, under the tree, our tree. The tree with the leaves that spread to the sun like helping hands. The tree with the tall trunk and cool shade.

"It's hot," I complained, fanning myself with the back of my hand, the mid-August sun beating down from the unforgiving sun.

Mimi stood up. Her long dark hair draped down her back and her rosy face was pink.

Jared and I stared at her in confusion.

"We have been sitting here all day, complaining about the heat. I want to go hiking into the woods. My mom was talking of a small stream she found while she was exploring the new hunting trails." And with that Mimi marched off.

Jared looked at me and I looked at Jared and we both stood up to follow.

Our tree stood on a hill looking over the dark, forbidding woods. Those trees were black and tall in a way that our tree was

Virginia was living in Hoboken, New Jersey, when her story appeared in the July/August 2010 issue of Stone Soup.

not. Those trees rose like mountains until they seemed to scrape the glaring cloudless sky. They whispered about some untold secret when the wind passed, rattling together with a sound like bones.

It was for this reason that I stopped at the forest's edge. Long, thick, parched stems of grasses pressed up against my legs. A small red-and-black ladybug was crawling, ever so slowly, up one of the stems. It reached the top, lost its footing and fell.

"Emma, hurry up!" Mimi's voice was impatient and I could see her far ahead, through the trees. Her yellow summer dress stood out like a ghost against the dark trunks and I hurried to catch up.

We followed no path in particular. The forest floor was carpeted with leaves, which had fallen in the late summer drought, making the ground crunchy and hard to see. There were no birds and no small animals. No, they had all fled, searching for water somewhere else.

We reached the place. A place where the trees were green and lush and the grass sang. When a gust of wind blew, it sang of joy and happiness and life. There were rocks beyond the grass that led to a river. Not a stream, as described by Mimi's mother, but a rushing, swishing, pouring river. The water was a clear, beautiful, turquoise blue.

Mimi flung off her shoes and ran to dip her toes into the water and Jared followed not too far after. We hadn't seen this much water in a long time. My feet dipped under the cold surface and felt the hard, round pebbles of the riverbed between their toes.

Jared gasped and I looked up.

On the opposite shore was a woman. She was tall and slender. Her hair was thick and hung in ringlets around her face. She wore a white dress though her feet were bare. But the most amazing part of her beauty was she seemed to emanate a faint, silvery glow.

I glanced sideways at Jared and his mouth was hanging open. I longed to shut it and ask this wonderful lady to forgive his rudeness, but I didn't.

She opened her mouth and the word came out like a tumbling waterfall, fluent and enchanting. "Come."

Jared stepped forward as if under a spell. Somehow, he crossed the river and stood beside her. She grabbed him by the arm and ran with a wonderful grace.

Mimi screamed and ran after her, sloshing through the racing river. The woman paused just inside the trees and looked back. Her eyes grew dark and hard, they seemed to grow bigger and bigger until they swallowed everything else. The world tipped under me and all was quiet.

My eyes fluttered open and I was back under the tree, our tree, with Mimi and Jared beside me. Something was different and I looked up to see the sky open in a torrential downpour.

They're Pigs!

by Adam Jacobs, age 11

IT WAS A BEAUTIFUL morning in California. The ocean sparkled... the trees were a lush green... what a perfect time for the loud, unwelcome buzz of the alarm clock. Ryan got out of bed and shut the thing off. A little too suddenly, he decided, as he began to grow dizzy and weary. He staggered across the room to the door. He needed breakfast. Now. *What day is it, anyway?* he wondered. The calendar said it was Thursday. Thursday! Thursday was wake-up-the-family-in-a-weird-and-obnoxious-way day! He had been waiting for this day since... well, last Thursday! Quick as lightning, he got dressed and ran downstairs, grabbed his special bucket, and dashed into his parents' bedroom.

And sure enough, there they were. Two little bumps under the sheets. He walked up next to them, leaned way over the bed, tipped the bucket over, and out came pounds upon pounds of cold, wet mud. But he didn't hear surprised screams. He didn't hear a sharp gasp. What he heard was an "Ahhh... thank you son..."

Adam was living in Brooklyn Park, Minnesota, when his story appeared in the January/February 2007 issue of Stone Soup.

"Dad?" Ryan gulped. "What did you say?"

"I said, *'Thank you son!'*"

"Can you say that one more time?"

"If you want me to…"

"Can I have that in writing?" Ryan grinned.

"I just said thank you, OK?" he cried. "It's nice to wake up to something cool and refreshing once in a while!"

"That *was* very nice of you, dear," said his mom. And slowly, the bump underneath the sheets began to make its way towards the head of the bed. It reached the end of the sheets, then out popped a round, pink nose, two little black eyes, four little legs, and one curly little tail. All in all, a chubby little pig popped out instead of the tall slender figure of Ryan's mother. Ryan wasn't grinning anymore.

"Mom?"

"Yes, dear?"

"What on earth is wrong with you?"

"What's wrong with her? Why son, that's very, very rude!" His father poked his head out from under the sheet to reveal yet another pig, just as fat as the last one.

"Are you guys, you know, really there? Or is this some kind of joke?" Ryan said.

"What are you talking about?" The pigs were definitely moving their mouths to form the words. Freaky. Then the one that was talking and acting just like his mom looked at the clock. "Oh my goodness! It's eight o'clock already! We're going to be late for work!"

And before Ryan could stop them, both pigs ran out of the bedroom, grabbed some documents, and headed out the door. Two pigs driving a car in the middle of rush hour. Oh dear.

He had to do *something*. But what? He could take the bus and meet his parents at their workplace and stop them from being seen… but the nearest bus stop was over a mile away. Then again, the nearest bike and equipment rental was just down the street. And they happen to specialize in motor scooters. Yeah. That would work. Just one more obstacle in his way. The s-i-s-t-e-r. Anxiously, he knocked on the door to his sister's bedroom. "Sis? I've got to go... to, uh, take a special summer-school class that I forgot to tell you about... uh, really... and I'm going to be gone for a while so I thought I should tell you. Bye!"

"Wait just one minute there, buster! You promised to make me breakfast today!"

"Really? Well, not now, OK? I'm already very late! Is it OK if I make you lunch instead?"

"*No!*" She pulled open the door. And out stepped another chubby little pig, complete with lipstick and a bad hairdo.

"Not you too!" Ryan ran downstairs and bolted outside, entirely forgetting his promise to make her breakfast.

FIFTEEN MINUTES LATER, he was on the bus, riding the twenty miles between his house and his parents' workplace. He knew he shouldn't have left his sister like that, but he also knew that if he had spent the time to make her a couple of waffles and an iced glass of orange juice there would have been no chance of bringing his parents home before they were seen.

And, he thought, what would have happened then? Would they have been captured and placed on some farm out in the middle of nowhere? Has someone seen them already? And will they even make it to work without crashing into something, with those little piggy hooves of theirs on the steering wheel? He tried not to think about all the ifs and maybes, but they kept nagging at him. What if it really was a prank that his family was pulling? What if this was all just a nightmare? Yes, that's it. It's just a bad dream. And he was really still snuggled in bed, safe and sound. And it was a Monday. Yeah! It wasn't even wake-up-the-family-in-a-weird-and-obnoxious-way day after all!

The bus came to a halt. It was time to get off. He got out of the bus and stepped onto a large parking lot before an ominous black building. He was there.

The bus pulled away and Ryan was left alone in the lot. It was filled with thousands of shiny cars but there wasn't a single person in sight. And it was impossible to see anything the size of a pig behind those rows and rows of automobiles. Not to mention a *talking* pig carrying a bunch of documents.

But then... what was that over there? He squinted towards the entrance to the building. Yes, there were definitely two little pink dots making their way across the sidewalk. He had to get them away from there before they were seen. Ryan began to run as fast as he could. The pigs were too far to catch in time. If he was lucky, there would be no one standing next to the entrance and he could catch them inside. He came to a halt on the sidewalk as he saw his parents inside through the glass door, talking to a tall man in a white suit. Ryan's head began to spin. What would happen now? Would the man call the pound? Would his parents be slaughtered?

Without thinking, he burst into the building. *"Stop!"* he said. He could hear some distant murmurs in front of him, the concerned voices of his parents, mixed with the shouts of angry workers. His eyes went out of focus. Everything became a blur. He screamed as loud as he could, *"No!"* The word echoed into the back of his head.

"No..."

AND THEN HE awoke. He saw his parents hovering over him, concerned looks on their faces. "Ryan?" They were both in their normal human form. "Ryan, did you have a bad dream?" his mother said.

"Yeah... I guess..." he said. The concerned look vanished and was replaced with a stern frown.

"And can you tell me why there's mud all over our bed, young man?"

The Last Dragon

by Veronica Engler, age 13

I GAZE OUT ACROSS the valley from my perch on the old, gray cliff. I watch a band of knights ride toward me, scarlet flags embossed with white lions flying defiantly in the light breeze. They are followed by a crowd of villagers eager to view my slaying. I close my eyes for a moment, digging deep inside my fiery heart, and then I lift my head, letting a flame twenty yards long stream from my mouth.

I see the knights look up, pointing at me, and I can hear the word shouted and whispered from each human's lips. *Dragon.* I spread my wings, each the span of twenty feet and cloaked in deep sapphire and sparkling silver. I rise up, my great snakelike body impressive in the misty morning air. With my hawk's vision, I find the lead knight and fix upon him the glare of my color-shifting eyes and let loose another flame. *Dragon.*

The villagers begin to shout, as do the knights, and a few of both begin to turn back. I smile, revealing teeth sharp as swords. I turn and begin down the mountainside, planning to meet the

Veronica was living in Gilbert, Arizona, when her story appeared in the September/October 2005 issue of Stone Soup.

slaughter party at its base.

As I walk, my wings pulsing and my tail lashing against protruding stones, shattering them into a thousand flying pieces, I think about the cause of this confrontation. I have done nothing. Nothing—it is merely my size and my power that frightens them into the thought that I must be annihilated. But really, I am nothing compared to some dragons. Like Keicro, with his beautiful amber skin and deep crimson wings he seemed to have the sunset painted onto his scales...

I shut out the thought, gritting my teeth into a grotesque grin. After what they did to Keicro, after what those humans did to my family—to condemn me to death for an imagined crime—after the mass slaughter of those I loved...

I glare ahead, the crowd of people coming into view. I will think of my family as I battle—of the great scaly beasts who dropped from the skies like stones and the blank eyes of those who had already passed into the next world while swords flashed like silver death. Banners flew in tatters as arrows rained down on the remainder of us. Yes, I will think of them in battle and it will give me strength.

I step into the valley and the knights step back while the villagers flee to hide behind the boulders scattered throughout the lush green vegetation of the valley. I let loose a ground-shaking roar, my rage echoing in each vibration. The leader of the knights slides off his horse and draws his sword, stepping bravely to fight me. I glower at him through the morning mist, my eyes shifting from smoky shadows to glittering turquoise to intense amethyst. The knight glares back at me with bronze eyes. Bronze eyes I recognize. Suddenly I see a scene play before my eyes. Keicro lies on the blood-stained ground, eyes closed, his last breath escaping his lips. A knight pulls his sword from my brother's heaving side and as he turns I can see his eyes. They are a gleaming bronze. The knight turns away and wipes his blade on the grass.

I cannot control the rage boiling inside me and release it in a stream of fire. The warrior dodges and narrowly avoids the licking red and gold. I snort with annoyance. I lift my wings, spreading them so wide they block the rising sun, throwing the cowering humans into darkness. I roar and beat my wings. I rise into the air, feeling my ally the wind help me mount the sky. I take a deep breath, feeling the winged beast stir in my blood. I feel at ease off the ground, the spaciousness of the air. I open my eyes and turn to the knight. I swoop down on him, seeing nothing but the man who murdered my brother.

The bronze-eyed warrior takes a swipe at me with his sword, but I knock it away and catch him in my iron claws, pinning him against the grass. He looks up at me. I smile, my teeth white and long.

How does it feel? I want to ask him. How does it feel to be small and helpless? How does it feel? Does it feel terrible, like a cold that races through your blood and chills your heart? Do you feel the terror?

I look deep into his eyes, and I am surprised. In this man's eyes—this man, who I have hated for years for the death of my brother—I see fear, not for himself but for his family. I am drawn into his mind by my natural power of telepathy and I see a woman with blond hair falling in waves down her back and by her feet a small human. The small human only comes up to the woman's knee and its eyes are bronze also, curiosity and innocence swirling within. And then I see the woman, obviously the knight's mate, lying on a bed, sweating from fever and crying out. I see his little girl crying, afraid for her mother.

I stare at this man and realize that, while I have lost my family, he is in danger of losing his. I try to convince myself that it is what he deserves, but I just cannot. No one—no one—should ever have to lose their loved ones. Never.

I lift my claw to release him but as I do, I feel a pain in my foreleg and turn to see another knight attacking me. I roar and bat him away, but another knight attacks me and then another and another. Suddenly I am surrounded by yelling humans wielding swords and sinking them into my flesh. I roar and swipe at them, but they keep coming back at me.

I try to burn them with another flame but my aim is compromised as a human manages to pierce my stomach, and I bellow as I go down. And then they are all upon me, the noise and screaming bringing me back to the bloodbath they initiated so many years ago. I see my family members fall before my eyes and realize that it is now my turn to die...

Suddenly the onslaught stops and all is quiet. I hear the breathing of the horses, the pounding hearts of the villagers watching. I hear the wind whispering to me in the voices of my lost family and I ease my eyes open. Standing before me is the knight with the bronze eyes. He takes a step toward me cautiously, and when I do not try to cremate him, he takes another step.

Soon he is right beside me. Carefully, he lays his hand on my face, looking into my eyes. He whispers something to me, but I cannot understand his language. Instead I look into his eyes and there is a question. I think a moment, and then nod.

Yes, I think, feeling that I could cry if I had not exhausted my tears years ago. I am the last dragon.

He leans forward and lays his head on my cheek and whispers again. I cannot understand the words, but I understand the feeling of sorrow and the rhythm of the words is so comforting. I close my eyes and I see Keicro. He says something, though I cannot hear him. A white light engulfs me and the faces of my family appear around me. They are all saying the same thing and at last I can hear the words.

"Come home, Liljuka. Come home to your family."

I smile, tears falling down my cheeks as I fly to meet them. I do not have to be alone anymore. I do not have to be angry in that lonely existence ever again.

THE KNIGHT STANDS, looking down at the ground. He is too late. The sun reflects off azure scales in a mockery of life, but the dragon is already gone. The knight wipes the wetness from his eyes and turns back to his men. He walks silently to his horse, mounts and rides back toward the village.

The villagers and knights watch him leave with silent confusion. This should be a moment of triumph—of celebration—but the air is weighted down with sorrow and regret. The great dragon lies still, lifeless and sad. Soon the crowd begins to leave, trying to escape this scene.

THE BRONZE-EYED knight plods along on his horse, thoughts of his wife and child swirling in his mind. He sighs so heavily it is almost a sob. He feels a cool breeze on his back and looks up. The morning mist is almost completely gone, but as he looks up at the sun he sees a shadowy image pass through the remaining mist. The shape is familiar...

He smiles when he sees a flash of blue and silver through the haze.

Dragon.

Dreams

by Justin Mai, age 12

BERG WOKE UP for the seventh time this week in a cold sweat. That same dream had invaded his subconscious again, the dream where he is in the jungle, where through the thick brush he can make out a light, like a campfire. And there is also the rhythmic throbbing of voices and the steady beat of crude drums being pounded. Each time he had come closer to the fire only to wake up when he is right about to part the ferns that separated him from the circle of people around the fire.

Normally, Berg, being a sensible and down-to-earth kind of person, would have dismissed the dreams, but this was no normal dream, it was very vivid, so vivid that, sometimes, he forgot whether that reality was just a dream, or the dream was a reality.

I ought to see a therapist about this, he thought uneasily while climbing out of his rickety old bed, careful not to wake his fellow orphans who were sleeping in the large "nursery."

Berg climbed down the cold, metal steps that led to the large common room that dominated his orphanage. From there he

Justin was living in Edmond, Oklahoma, when his story appeared in the March/April 2005 issue of Stone Soup.

turned to a hallway that led to the kitchen where his favorite nun was sure to be working on making the children's breakfasts.

"Well hello, Howard, what are you doing up so early?"

"The dreams," he said simply, while Sister Amy nodded knowingly. "Also, I've asked you, please call me Berg."

The homely nun rolled her eyes and continued cracking eggs into a large bowl. "I'll call you by the name this orphanage gave you, not some nickname you made up."

There was a brief pause, broken by Berg asking hopefully, "Any news?"

Amy looked at him sadly and said, "No, I'm afraid not."

They were talking about the news of Berg's origin. He had been given to the orphanage five years ago, and ever since then he had been obsessed with learning about his past. The nuns did what they could, which was to ask other orphanages around the state if they remembered him, and to pray, of course.

"Darn it," he said, feeling the familiar suffocating grip of hopelessness tighten around his body.

"Oh, don't worry," said Amy. "There's always Fleming's Domicile for the Destitute," she said, squeezing his arm and giving him a wink. He laughed. It was an old joke of theirs. When he had first come and expressed his desire to find out who his parents were, the first orphanage they checked said they had no record of him. It was then that Amy had come and consoled him and said that it was always the most strangely named place that held all the information you needed. They had spent the rest of that afternoon making up different names for this unknown, strangely named orphanage, and Fleming's was his favorite.

Berg got up from the stool he was sitting on and walked out of the kitchen, flopping on a brown, bumpy couch in the commons. He had just gotten a wave of vertigo, that feeling when it seemed like nothing was real. He gripped his hand tightly on the couch armrest until it passed.

He looked around at the familiar settings of the large room. In the northeast corner there was a ping-pong table that would most certainly be used over a hundred times today. Lining the room were cushy armchairs and rather overstuffed couches, and in the southwest corner was a large bookcase.

Soon though, Berg's relaxation was broken by the sound of a large alarm clock and the thunder of feet stepping down the staircase. Like a large herd of cattle, the student body tromped through the commons and into the dining room, where breakfast was to be served. Berg got up shakily and walked over to where his two best friends were, near the back of the line, as usual.

"Hey, Clare, Nathan," said Berg when he reached them. Nathan nodded in recognition and Clare smiled happily, glad that all of her few friends were around her; Nathan only stuck his hands deep in his pockets and whistled a tuneless song.

Finally, when they had progressed through the line and were sitting at a table, Nathan asked, "So, dreams again?"

Berg smiled. He knew, of course. Nathan was the most normal and predictable person you could and probably ever would meet. It was for this that Berg had liked him so much. It was his normalcy that made him strange, because while everyone had their own unique style, Nathan had none. This in itself was a type of style that Nathan took special pride in.

"Yeah… They're getting much more vivid, ya know?" said Berg after much thought. Clare and Nathan both nodded wisely, although both were hoping that the strange nightmares that had settled on their friend's mind would simply go away.

There was an awkward silence, broken only by Clare looking down at her plate, sighing, as if to change the subject, and pushing it away. "Do they expect me to eat this? 'Cause I am not eating this," she declared, although there was never an answer. It was purely a rhetorical question, more like a ritual really. She looked disdainfully at the gray metal tray that held some sorry-looking eggs and piece of toast with a smidgen of jam on it. Then, as if accepting her fate, Clare picked up her plastic fork and grudgingly took a small bite of the egg.

The school bell was like an old woman, yelling at them

hoarsely, telling them to get to class, or suffer the consequences. Because every student knew what the consequences were, they all hurried. Clare and Berg had to part with Nathan as they went to the math class while he went to English for his first hour.

In math they were covering dimensional analysis and many students were having trouble. Just as the teacher was explaining, for the third time, how to multiply with exponents, the familiar feeling of vertigo came to Berg.

His desk seemed to flicker and waver, changing to a small bush and changing back again. The girl in front of him disappeared for a moment and then reappeared but with slightly greenish skin. Then sweat started beading on Berg's forehead; his nose began to bleed. He could hear the distant throbbing of drums. Without noticing it, Berg fell out of his desk. The teacher suddenly looked up to see him writhing on the floor. With a shriek of surprise and fear she came to him and roughly shook him. Almost immediately Berg opened his dark eyelids, but not to reveal the usual brown irises.

His entire eyes were like windows. In them the children and the teacher saw golden beaches, tigers at play, wild jungles and strange, exotic animals. Soon though, his eyes faded back to their usual luster, but holding a very confused and pained expression.

The room was suddenly very silent, the teacher in mid-shake, the students with their mouths agape. The silence was broken by Clare's overly loud voice. "Did you guys see that?" she said in her usual blunt and straightforward manner. That seemed to snap everyone back to reality.

The teacher stood up, and in a very dignified manner began straightening her habit. She then looked gravely at Berg and said in a very quiet voice that betrayed how scared she actually was, "I think you'd better get to the infirmary."

Berg slowly got up, making sure to use his desk for leverage. Then, silently, he walked out of the room. Once out, he leaned heavily on the wall. He looked silently at his hands, touched his head, and wriggled his toes until he was completely sure he had not broken anything. The pain had been excruciating. It felt like being digested; his skin burned, and his bones cracked, and yet, there didn't seem to be any lasting harm done to him. Thanking God for the miracle, Berg resolved to head over to the nurse's office anyway. Just as he passed through the hallway that led to the commons though, the vertigo came again.

It seemed as if this time it came with a vengeance, furious that Berg had gotten away last time unscathed. He collapsed and his nose began to bleed profusely. He found that instead of tile, his hands were resting on muddy dirt, and also, that the pain had seemed to go away. A centipede crawled over his outstretched hand, and when Berg looked up, he wasn't in his orphanage anymore. He was in the jungle. The jungle of his dreams.

Although Berg was usually a very cautious person, none of this struck him as odd. He slowly got up and walked carefully to the clearing that he could see through the wild brush. The sound of drums pounding in his ears, he pushed aside ferns and tree branches and he came to the clearing. Instantly the music stopped. There, right in the middle of the clearing, was a small fire. Resting near it was an old man, dressed in what might have been a shaman's robe, and wrinkled beyond compare. Behind him some old huts that had evidently not been used for decades, and were falling into decay.

Almost as if sensing his presence, the old man looked up sharply and looked at Berg with surprisingly piercing and alert eyes. Upon seeing him, the man seemed satisfied and his gaze softened. Slowly, as if he had the weight of the world on his shoulders, the old man stood up and approached him. As he walked, Berg could see glimpses of his school. He knew they were in the hallway, but, at the same time they were in South Africa.

Finally, after what seemed like a million lifetimes, they met eye-to-eye. Berg tried to think of questions, but all thought had left his mind completely.

SISTER AMY WAS walking down the hall when she saw Berg. He was face down on the floor, his arm stretched behind his back. Around his head was a small pool of blood.

"Howard!" she yelled, falling upon him, cradling his head, and gently trying to shake him out of his trancelike state. When it became obvious that her efforts were useless, she bundled him up in her arms and rushed to the nurse's office.

SUDDENLY, JUST as it seemed that the old man was going to speak, Berg felt a jarring explosion of pain in his body. Instantly, the jungle around him flickered to reveal the orphanage's white walls. He could feel hands on him but that didn't matter, only the pain did. Once again, it was like a giant stomach grinding him up. He could feel his body being ripped apart at the seams. When he finally did open his eyes, it was as if the worlds had been spliced. The floor was made of dirt, the walls were white, the white stone of his orphanage. Around the walls were ferns that seemed to be two-dimensional and crucifixes just like them. Then, Berg didn't have time to see the other strange things in the room, he only saw black.

When Berg did look up, he was in the jungle with the old man. Only instead of being calm like he was before, he seemed to be concentrating very hard.

His earlier shyness having left him, Berg opened up in a flurry of questions. "What am I doing here? How did I get here? Where are we?! Who are you?!" He said it all quickly, in one breath.

The old man, his concentration disrupted, could only look at him, grimace and grunt, "No questions ... Your world's too strong. It's trying to break through... I gotta... keep you here."

Berg could only gape, open-mouthed, until the old man relaxed and settled into a crouching position.

"Now, as for your first question, you are here to do a service to your great-great-great-great-great-great-great-grandfather."

Berg opened his mouth, he was about to open up with another

round of questions, but the old man quickly shushed him.

"You got here, through me, and we are in the spirit world," continued the old man. "Also, I am called Darakai," he added as an afterthought.

Berg sat very still for a little while, as if digesting the information he had been given. Finally, he looked up solemnly at Darakai and said, "What would you have me do?"

The old man grinned, then smiled, then laughed out loud, a loud, booming laugh that continued for a long time. After he had finished, he wiped his eyes and looked up at Berg. "You can't believe how long I've been waiting for someone to say that."

"NOW, DON'T WORRY!" said Darakai an hour and a half later. "You are a natural, believe me," he continued.

All Berg could do was nod numbly and ask, "You were really taken as a slave? And that leaf was all that stopped you from living in South Africa?"

Darakai nodded solemnly, "Yes, now, we begin. Remember, once you fold it back, it will disrupt the flow of time. You might black out for a while."

Berg nodded and asked, "And when I come to, it will be as if all of this never happened?"

Darakai said, "Yes," and he drew a bag of greenish powder from one of his belt pouches. The fire had since died down and was now a pile of embers, but when Darakai threw a pinch of the powder into it, the flames sprang up, abnormally long. As instructed, Berg looked deeply into the fire and tried to clear his mind.

The changes were gradual, but they happened all the same. The settings around him seemed to melt away, to be replaced by a starry sky. One small, insignificant light seemed to be rushing toward him. Soon he could see the familiar planet Earth, surrounding his field of vision. He kept rushing toward it until he could make out all of the continents. However, he noticed that once he concentrated on something, he could see it perfectly.

He could see a butterfly on North America and the energies it was creating that would soon form a tropical storm in Japan. He could see two dictators shaking hands and the country that would soon be conquered by their combined force. And he could see the fateful fern that his great-great-great-great-great-great-great-grandfather had tried to hide behind when the slavers had come. He could see the one leaf that had been folded over, thus betraying Darakai's position. And, with very tender care, Berg flew down to it, to the scene that had been frozen in place by Darakai's specially made powder, and with gentle care, he folded the leaf back, and then he only saw white.

IT WAS DARK when Burgta woke up to dreams of a large building and white children. As he walked out through the cool African night he saw his friend, Nakai. Nakai looked up from the fire he was putting out to see Burgta walking toward him.

"What is wrong?" he asked. Burgta just shook his head and replied simply. "Nothing, just... dreams."

In the Knights' Absence

by Emma Kilgore Hine, age 12

KYTHIA AWOKE to the sound of trumpets announcing her father's departure. She grunted and sat up abruptly, stretching stiff muscles. She had wished to speak with her father, Sir Farlan, before he and his knights left the castle to assist their fellow countrymen in battle. Kythia knew that if more troops weren't sent to help Queen Jocunda all of their kingdom of Naranth would be overrun by the power-hungry Rylions. Still, she wished her father had had time to plead her cause to her mother, Lady Amaria. Amaria wanted a daughter who would embroider tapestries, regally order servants to do her bidding, and wear elaborate gowns of silk and brocade. Kythia herself wanted to be a hero, someone portrayed in tapestries. She wanted to wear mail and carry a sword, and save all of Naranth. All Sir Farlan wanted was for his family to be content, and therefore it was always easy to enlist his help in halting Amaria's next lecture.

Kythia sighed. Now there was no prolonging the inevitable tirade. Her mother had caught her on her palfrey, tilting (or trying

Emma was living in Austin, Texas, when her story appeared in the July/August 2004 issue of Stone Soup.

THE STONE SOUP BOOK

to) at a quintain. The poor horse was bewildered and jumped at the slightest sound. Amaria had let out such an unladylike war cry as to spook the horse, meant only for pleasure, into throwing its passenger, and the glint in the noble lady's eyes threatened hell to pay. Kythia stood, wincing as her sore limbs stretched, and limped to the five-foot-tall mirror that had been her thirteenth birthday present. She tossed her waist-length hair, admiring the way the auburn tresses caught the light, then, grimacing, reached for the forest green gown that supposedly brought out the color of her already striking hazel eyes. Although the dress was stunning, she knew she'd look better in armor.

THAT MORNING (after the lecture at breakfast) Kythia endured dancing lessons, then embroidery two of her most hated activities. Nothing was worse than what came after the three-course midday meal, though: fittings. She was making her appearance at court in April, as did every other fifteen-year-old of high blood. The only pleasant part of this trip would be meeting with Queen Jocunda. The Queen was everything Kythia wished to be. She was a warrior, yet could be a proper, beautiful lady when she wished. She was a superb horsewoman and the heroine of every ballad. Meeting her would be wondrous.

Kythia was suddenly brought back to reality as the beautiful aqua-colored gown, her mother's choice, was draped over her slim shoulders. She sighed and resigned herself to an eternity of measurements and servants' gossip.

"Did you hear that there's a chance of the Rylions attacking near here?"

"Oh, that's not true. You know that Sir Farlan would never let them past him."

"Word has it that battle was just a diversion, and their real motive is to take this castle and the lands around it."

Kythia had heard this theory several times, and had yet to believe it. It would be exciting, though—trumpets blaring, banners waving just beyond the window. Oh, glory, maybe Queen

Jocunda would even lead the rescue...

That was odd. Kythia was sure she had just heard trumpets, even war cries. She shook her head, trying to clear it of what was obviously her imagination.

Then her mother, Amaria, dashed into the room and cried that, yes, there was a Rylion attack and the knights were gone, fighting miles away! This time, the gossip was correct.

That was when panic broke loose. Serving women shrieked and ran about. Villagers had already begun to enter the castle, the safest place around. Kythia maneuvered through it all, trying to reach the battlements. Her heart hammered; her hair flew out of place as she, still in her fine gown, scrambled to where she could help defend her people and her home. She couldn't let her mother and servants die or be captured. As she ran, she issued orders for vats of hot oil, bows and arrows, and as many spears as they had. She grabbed a boy about her age and gave him a message to take as quickly as possible to the nearest estate: We're under attack, and the men are gone. Please, help.

KYTHIA STOOD at the battlements clutching a bow expertly in one hand and felling enemies below as fast as she could fire. She'd secretly learned archery as a child, and was a fair shot. The most stalwart of the servants, men and women, assisted her, and the rest were huddled with Amaria in the most protected rooms.

Load. Fire. Watch her victim fall. Load. Fire. Kythia worked herself into a rhythm. She shut her mind to the screams of those she killed in self-defense, although she knew they would haunt her dreams.

A pain-filled shriek forced her to look beside her. One of the gossips that had been fitting her dress had fallen, struck by a deadly arrow. Blood spurted from her, showering the cold stone wall. Kythia took a moment to kneel beside her servant and gently close the eyes of the old woman.

Kythia's dress was ripped and hanging off one shoulder: the height of impropriety. Her hair was loose and tangled and tinted with soot. Her face was streaked with sweat, blood, and dirt. Yet Kythia was beautiful, wild and willful, standing in the battlements and crying out against all who defied her. She grinned; Lady Amaria would swoon with shock to see her daughter like this.

AFTER IT WAS all over Kythia sat in her spacious apartments and thought about the entire incident. They had won; serving women and one noble girl had held their own against a troop from the greatest army in the realm until proper warriors could be summoned. Perhaps an angel was with her, watching over her; perhaps it was just pure luck. Anyhow, she and the servants had done it, and Kythia was proud.

A knock at the door startled her out of her reverie. She jumped, and before she could respond the door opened and admitted Amaria and—someone. This woman was tall, slim, and muscular, with jet black hair and brilliant violet eyes. She carried a sword at her side and wore mail so beautiful as to astound even Amaria. She stepped forward and said in a throaty, commanding voice, " I am Jocunda. Am I correct in assuming that you, Kythia, are responsible for the defeat of the Rylion troop?"

Kythia, nervous at being addressed by her sovereign and heroine, reverently whispered, " Yes, Your Majesty. I am Kythia, and I suppose you could say that I am responsible."

AFTER JOCUNDA had addressed Kythia and her mother for several minutes she took her leave, promising to speak more at the dawn. Amaria, at her daughter's questioning glance, responded, "Her Majesty the Queen was visiting a nearby estate, and, when messengers arrived, requesting help with the wounded, she made haste to accompany the party.

"Kythia..." Her tone was soft, shy, forgiving. "I'm proud of you. Oh, Kythia, I'm so proud."

Mr. Larson's Library

by Jordan Coble, age 12

TWELVE-YEAR-OLD EMILY hobbled down the stairs, rubbing her tired hazel eyes. She collapsed onto a chair in the breakfast room, clutching a book in her hand.

"How was *The Lake?*" an old man asked, nodding toward the book. Wispy gray hair adorned the sides and back of his head like a garland, but the top was smooth and shiny as a crystal ball.

Holding back a yawn, Emily swept a lock of reddish-brown hair out of her face and replied, "It was really good, Grandpa. It doesn't have a lot of suspense or action in it, but it was really descriptive. I could picture myself right on the lake in the story."

"I can tell you liked it, Emily, or else you would not have stayed up all night to finish it," Emily's grandfather, Mr. Larson, said, chuckling. Mr. Larson owned a little library on Main Street, and his granddaughter enjoyed previewing books before he placed them on his shelves. Mr. Larson called this job a "book tester."

"Is it really good for Emily's health to stay up so late reading

Jordan was living in Camino, California, when her story appeared in the July/August 2009 issue of Stone Soup.

THE STONE SOUP BOOK

these books?" questioned Emily's mother, her pretty brownish-green eyes the exact image of Emily's.

"Of course it's good for her!" Mr. Larson exclaimed. "Reading is very good for your soul."

Frowning, Emily's mother poured a bowl of cereal for her daughter and handed it to her.

"I got a new shipment of books yesterday, Emily," Mr. Larson said excitedly. Emily suddenly perked up and her eyes sparkled like diamonds. Her cheeks, dusted with freckles like cinnamon sprinkles, glowed with excitement.

"Really?" she asked excitedly. "May I test them out?"

"Of course," Mr. Larson promised. "The box of books is at the library. We'll go right after you finish your breakfast."

Cramming large spoonfuls of Cheerios into her mouth, Emily said through her bites, "I'll be done in five minutes."

EMILY AND HER GRANDFATHER were walking hand in hand down the sidewalk. Orange, red, and yellow leaves twirled in the chilly November breeze like beautiful ballerinas. Emily's mittened hand covered her icy nose as they briskly traipsed through the streets until they reached Mr. Larson's Library.

Unlocking the glass door, Mr. Larson swung it open and ushered Emily into the building. The cozy, one-room library was filled with hundreds of books on beautiful, smooth oak shelves. Behind the counter sat a large cardboard box. Emily imagined herself riffling through the pages of each one, smelling the crisp scent of brand-new books.

"Pull out the scissors from the desk drawer, Emily, so we can open this," Mr. Larson said, kneeling down beside the box. Pulling open the drawer, Emily's hands closed around the scissors. Then she saw *it*.

It was a stunning, maroon leather-bound book with gold lettering on the cover. The pages did not look new, for they were torn in some spots, yellowed, and smelled musty. The title was simply *The Story*. Emily thought she had never seen a more beautiful book.

"I've never seen this book in your library before. May I preview it?" she asked her grandfather hopefully.

His faint eyebrows frowned in worry. "Pay no mind to it," Mr. Larson said. "It's just an old magic book."

"It's a magic book?" breathed Emily. "Oh, Grandpa! Please let me read it!"

"Magic books can be very dangerous," cautioned Mr. Larson. "I cannot allow any harm to come upon my only grandchild." There was a slight warmness in his voice, but at the same time Emily heard an authoritative strictness in it, too, so she didn't say another word about The Story.

THAT NIGHT, EMILY settled down in her bed to read the pile of books she had chosen from the box at her grandfather's library. The small tower included novels from her favorite author, chapter books from budding writers, and so on. But none of those interested her, for underneath the heap of books sat *The Story*. It had taken some careful maneuvering to sneak it into her selection of books, but she had succeeded, and as she opened up *The Story*, the trouble she had gone to seemed worth it.

The Story was the most amazing book she had ever read. Somehow, it combined all styles of writing: fiction, drama, comedy, and more, into one pleasing paragraph after another. She devoured the thick book, and soon forgot where she was. The way the words were woven together and the way the author described settings and characters were magical, but the true magic of the book was not yet revealed to her.

HER LAMP GLOWED softly like a firefly, penetrating the pitch-black night outside. Rain pelted down on the roof and the harsh wind whipped the tree limbs around, the boughs making a scraping noise against the window. Eerie shadows from the gnarled, clawing arms of trees cast menacing silhouettes on the walls. It was midnight, and Emily had fallen asleep on her bed, her auburn hair spread out on the soft pillow. *The Story* sat beside her, the light shining on its pages. This is where the magic began.

Wiry, leafy vines began to grow from the pages, coiling around each other like a snake. They climbed up the walls, cloaking the white paint in dark green masses. More plants, including exotic flowers and tiny saplings, began to sprout from the pages, crowding to move out of *The Story* and into the real world.

But plants were only the beginning of the problem. The array of botany was followed by various species of animals, including lions, tigers, and even a few monkeys. By this point, Emily could not have stayed asleep with the grunts, roars, and other noises that filled the air.

When she awoke, her mouth dropped open and her face went pale as she saw what was before her. Her eyes swept the room, looking for the source of this stampede of nature, although she already knew the origin. *The Story* was the only possible thing that could have caused this havoc, and when she looked down at the book, she saw she was right. More plants and animals were erupting from the spine like a volcano, adding more chaos than there already was.

Emily's stomach knotted up in fear, her dread mainly caused by the ferocious-looking big cats. But her anxiety of the punishment for disobedience propelled her on, assisting her to gather up enough courage to slip out of her cocoon of blankets and onto the carpeted floor.

Bravely marching up to a monkey, she ordered in a somewhat quivering voice, "Get back in the book." The little primate yanked her hair and sped away. Emily huffed angrily. The little rascal seemed to be laughing at her!

Trying not to show her frustration at how uncooperative the monkey was, she concentrated her effort on other things. Emily desperately tried to pull the vines off the wall, but they seemed to be tugging against her, leaving painful red marks on her hands. She attempted to carry a baby lion back into the pages, despite her fear. The coarse fur of the wild feline brushed against her hands and she pushed, shoved, and hauled the big cat beside *The Story*, but he simply walked away. Each plan she tried thereafter that didn't work made her feel more and more discouraged.

Her grandfather was constantly on her mind as well. I will get in so much trouble if he finds out, she thought. She remembered his caution from earlier that day: "Magic books can be very dangerous." He had warned her about the book. Now it was too late.

Or so Emily thought.

The door suddenly swung open. There stood Mr. Larson. Despite her worry about the punishment she would receive, Emily had never been so grateful to see her grandpa. He calmly strode to the bed and picked up *The Story*. Emily watched with great interest as he carried the book to each plant, and individually tore each from the wall or ground with his strong hands and placed it back into the pages. They disappeared. As the plants began to disappear, so did the animals. They walked to the book themselves, as if knowing they had to go back. By simply putting a paw onto a page, they were whisked back into *The Story*.

In only five minutes Mr. Larson had swiftly and easily restored the room back to normal. Emily sighed with relief but then remembered she had a consequence to face. She braced herself, but her grandpa simply closed the cover of the book and left the room without muttering a single word.

As soon as he left, thoughts were swimming in Emily's mind. Why didn't Grandpa punish me? How did he know I needed help? What would have happened if he hadn't come? She sat on her bed, pondering these and other questions, until the sun began to peek over the horizon and she finally fell asleep.

THE NEXT MORNING, Mr. Larson, Emily's mother, and her father were sitting around the breakfast table, drinking coffee and chatting together.

"Good morning, Emily," her mother said as the preteen girl sat down. "Why, you look exhausted!" She frowned at Mr.

Larson. "She really needs to stop reading books at night. I am telling you, it is bad for her health!" Emily's mother and father were obviously unaware of the bizarre and terrifying situation that had happened the night before.

"I got a second shipment of books early this morning," Mr. Larson said, ignoring Emily's mother. "Would you like to come over to the library to look at them?"

Emily had never wanted to stay home as badly as she did today. The terror of the midnight experience still haunted her, and she was apprehensive about any other book she might read. But she did not want her parents to know about *The Story*; they'd think she was insane or lying, so she mumbled, "All right, I guess."

A SHORT TIME LATER, Emily and her grandfather sat in Mr. Larson's Library, each lost in their own thoughts about the situation last night. Silence blanketed the library, and except for the ticking of the clock on the wall, all was calm.

"How did you know I had the magic book? How did you know I needed help? Why didn't you punish me?" Emily suddenly asked, breaking the tranquil peacefulness that hung in the air.

"Well, let's begin with a short story," Mr. Larson said, leaning back in his chair. "There once lived a little boy whose grandfather owned a library on Main Street. One day, the little boy found a magic book and read it, despite his grandfather's warning. The book came to life that night, and the little boy had to figure out for himself how to get his bedroom back to normal. After that, the boy developed an appreciation and respect for magic. The young boy was very curious and inquisitive, not unlike yourself, Emily."

Even though no mention had been made about him, Emily knew the little boy in the story was Mr. Larson. Emily's grandfather had obviously been through the same experience as a child. That answered the first two questions. "But why didn't you punish me?" Emily asked.

"Will you ever read a magic book again?" Mr. Larson

inquired.

Shaking her head, Emily responded earnestly, "No!"

"Then do you need a punishment?" Mr. Larson queried.

"But I disobeyed you," Emily pointed out.

"I'm not one for punishments, I suppose," Mr. Larson replied, shrugging. They were silent again for a few more minutes, but then Emily had another question.

"Why do you still have *The Story?*" she wondered.

"Perhaps so my granddaughter can develop an appreciation and respect for magic," Mr. Larson said, giving Emily a smile and a wink.

CPSIA information can be obtained
at www.ICGtesting.com
Printed in the USA
FSOW02n1917100315
5559FS